MISS ROBINSON AND THE UNSUITABLE BARON

SOFI LAPORTE

Editor: Jessica Ryn
Proofreader: Stacey Ulferts
Cover Art: Covers and Cupcakes
ISBN: 978-3-9505190-9-9

CHAPTER ONE

iss Ellen Robinson, instructress at Miss Hilversham's Seminary for Young Ladies, was sitting in a stagecoach bound for London. A small dark head bumped against her upper arm in rhythm with the carriage as it rattled along the road.

"Ye have a beautiful child, there, missus," said the woman who sat across from her. She wore a shawl around her head and held a basket of turnips on her lap. She'd been talking the entire journey, and within an hour of meeting her, Ellen knew that her name was Henny Miller, married to a Tom Miller, with three grown children, and that she was on her way to London to visit her sister Jill, who was married to an innkeeper in Charing Cross Road.

The other travellers, a dour-looking gentleman and a soldier, looked out of the window. Henny had looked at Ellen as if expecting her to share her personal story, but Ellen had merely smiled.

The woman nodded at the sleeping child. "Looks just

like me John, when 'e was a baby. Same dark, thick curls. What a little angel. 'Ow old is 'e?"

"Four." Ellen had no idea how old Noni was. But four seemed as good a guess as any.

The woman pursed her lips. "A difficult age. No longer a babe, but not ready to work either. Always falling from one scrape to another. My advice is never to let 'im out of yer sight, lest 'e drowns 'isself in the rain barrel or the 'orse trough. They always do, ye know." The woman sniffed. "'Appened to me neighbour's boy the other day."

Ellen's head snapped up. "The poor child drowned in a horse trough?"

"Almost. My 'usband fished 'im out just in time."

Ellen breathed a sigh of relief. She lifted the arm that had fallen asleep, shook it and put it around the child's shoulders, raising him gently so that his feet rested on the seat and his head on her lap.

"Yer a good mama," the woman said approvingly.

Ellen smiled tightly.

She was as related to the child as a grasshopper was to a blackbird. She hadn't even known of Noni's existence until yesterday morning. He'd been standing on the porch of the seminary, a small trunk at his side, a letter tucked in the pocket of his coat, and his big black eyes filled with tears.

Someone had dropped him off and disappeared by the time Martha opened the door. Martha, the good soul, had taken him in, wiped his cheeks, and sat him down at the kitchen table, with a glass of warm milk and a plate of oat biscuits. Then she'd informed the headmistress, Miss Hilversham, that they had a new pupil.

Miss Hilversham was married to the Duke of

Rochford and should properly be called "Your Grace" and "Lady Rochford", but all the pupils and teachers at the seminary still called her "Miss Hilversham". The name stuck to her like glue. The school was named after her, and under her leadership it had developed a reputation for excellence. So she'd thought it wise to keep the name and persona of Miss Hilversham separate from that of the Duchess of Rochford.

"What on earth is this man thinking?" Miss Hilversham knitted her brows together as she perused the letter tucked into Noni's coat. "This Baron Trevesbury. Or is it Twiksbury? Terrible penmanship. Dumping the child on our porch like that. This is a seminary for young ladies, not a nursery for little children. Nor do we accept boys. Here, read this." She handed the letter to Ellen, frowning so deeply that her eyebrows touched the bridge of her nose.

The missive was difficult to read. It was smudged with tea stains, and what wasn't smeared was illegible. The child was called Undecipherable Name, and he was to receive schooling at Miss Hilversham's Seminary. Signed, Twillsbury, or some variation thereof, 11 Hanover Square.

Ellen shook her head. "It's barely legible. What shall we call him?" She squinted at the paper. "Does it say Noni? Is that an N or a V?"

Miss Hilversham pursed her lips. "Noni is a popular nickname for Giovanni." She peered again at the scrawled words. "It must be Giovanni Battista," she pronounced. "An excellent reminder that penmanship is not only important, but can be positively crucial in certain circumstances. Let's make sure we increase our calligraphy and penmanship lessons for all students. It would be unthinkable if any of our students left our school with such penmanship." She shuddered.

"But Giovanni Battista is an Italian name, isn't it?" A wrinkle formed between Ellen's eyebrows. "Did he come straight from the Continent?"

Both women looked at the child sitting at the table, crumbling biscuits. Martha took one, dipped it in the milk and held it out to him. A small smile appeared on his face as he ate it.

"What is your name, child?" Miss Hilversham asked, but the child made no response. "Noni?"

Again no response.

"Perhaps he doesn't speak English?" Ellen suggested.

Miss Hilversham sat down beside him. "Sei Giovanni?"

The child dipped the biscuit into his glass as if she hadn't spoken.

"Come ti chiami?"

The child stopped dipping the cookie and dropped his head.

Miss Hilversham's and Ellen's eyes met over his dark little head. He wasn't deaf, was he? Ellen picked up a small bell and rang it.

His head snapped up.

Not deaf.

There was a gleam of interest in his eyes. She gave him the bell. "This is a bell. I ring it to let the children know that class is about to start." She placed it in front of him. He tipped it with one finger. "Won't you tell me your name?" No answer. "Hm. Let's see. Maybe you could ring it twice for me?"

The child picked up the bell and rang it twice.

So he understood English very well. He just refused to speak.

Miss Hilversham rubbed the space between her eyebrows. "Come out with me for a moment, Ellen. Keep an eye on him, Martha, while we discuss this."

The women went into the office.

"This is an inconvenience," Miss Hilversham began. "What was that Terrisbury thinking? There are exactly five things wrong with this situation. First, to drop off a child like that, willy-nilly, without consulting me first. It is beyond words. Second, he's too young for our school; he's almost a baby. Third, he is a boy. Fourth. We won't be taking any more children of dastardly guardians who can't be bothered with their wards. They have taken responsibility for these children, and they should fulfil that responsibility. There's nothing that infuriates me more than guardians who ignore their charges." She tapped the table with a finger. "And finally, the child seems to need special attention, and none of my teachers here have the time or energy for that."

"Just out of interest, wasn't Rochford just such a dastardly guardian?" Ellen wore an innocent, wide-eyed expression. Miss Hilversham's husband, Marcus, the Duke of Rochford, had indeed been such a guardian who'd dumped off his ward Pen at the school and never bothered with her. He'd made up for this neglect, however, and ended up marrying the school's headmistress.

Miss Hilversham took off her glasses and suddenly looked much younger.

"He was. Of the most terrible sort, too." An affectionate smile flitted across her face, softening her features, then the stern look returned to her brow. "But that doesn't mean that we are a dumping ground for unwanted wards. It won't do us any good, and it won't do the world any good either. These men need to be taught that once they take on the responsibility of guardianship, they have to keep it." She pushed her metal-rimmed spectacles back onto her nose. "Which is why you will go and find this"— she glanced at the letter, wrinkling her nose—"Tillisbury at Hanover Square Eleven and return this lovely boy to him."

"I shall?" Ellen groaned. "But I have twenty badly written essays to mark, an engaging but instructive history lesson to develop, a literature exam to write, and an art excursion to plan."

"Don't worry, Ellen. Christine, our new teacher, can take care of most of it, as she has no work yet, except to look after our pupils in between classes."

Ellen knew the seminary's newest teacher was more than capable. She simply did not want to go to London, especially with a child she didn't know. "Can't Martha take the child?"

"And have you take over her work of looking after the house? Collecting everyone's chamber pots and clearing the grate? I think not." Miss Hilversham tapped her finger impatiently on the desk. "We need someone with authority to go. You are the best person for that. You must tell this man that the poor child does not need to be in a seminary for young ladies. What he needs is a mother."

Ellen swallowed as she thought. This was an inconvenience. On the other hand, a brief trip to London would allow her to visit her family. Jenny, her stepmother, had written about some trouble regarding Drake, the eldest in the family. They desperately needed her help and advice.

She could deliver the child to Hanover Square and then drop in for a quick visit. It had been too long since she'd seen them all.

"When would you like us to leave?"

"Immediately."

So it was that Ellen found herself on the coach from Bath to London with a little boy clinging to her as if she were his only anchor in the world.

CHAPTER TWO

*E*dmund Graves, Sixth Baron Tewkbury, had just told the biggest fib of his life—that he was married.

It was a white lie born of desperation, uttered in his Haymarket fencing club, and he hadn't thought much of it at first. But in the heat of the moment he couldn't think of anything better to say, and once he'd said it, it was done. It was a fabulous idea, and now he had to see it through to the bitter end.

He kept the muscles in his face still and stared squarely into the watery blue eyes of his friend Lord Dunstan Dobberham, whose jaw had dropped to the netherworld.

"Blimey! That's a bag of moonshine," he finally uttered, jabbing a finger at him. "You're bamming me."

He was, of course. Until a minute ago, he hadn't even been engaged. But now he was freshly and happily married and busy working on filling his nursery. Edmund shrugged nonchalantly and played with the ribbon of his quizzing glass. "I'm not."

It had all started with Dobberham roasting him for obsessing too much about fashion. Edmund had just fenced with him and taken off his mask. His valet, whom he'd taken with him, helped him change his linen and tighten the corset, which he'd taken off for fencing. He brushed Edmund's coat and whipped out a cloth to rub a smudge off his Wellington boots.

"You dandies really have nothing else on your minds but clothes, do you?" Dobberham made no effort to hide the contempt in his voice.

"I do a bit of fencing, too, in case you hadn't noticed." Edmund flicked away an imaginary speck of lint on his sleeve.

"Really, Tewkbury. You've taken this interest in fashion too far. It's become an unhealthy obsession. You need a woman, a wife, to help you snap out of it. You will feel much better; I speak from experience. It's obvious that bachelorhood doesn't suit you. Makes you strange, eccentric and weird in the head."

"Why, thank you," Edmund murmured. "I'll take that as a compliment."

"Oy, Tewkbury here needs to get himself a wife." Dobberham called to Rutherford, who was standing nearby, making practice moves with his foil. "We must help him. Do you know anyone?"

"Certainly. Will my sister do?" Rutherford joked. His sister was a spinster and a bluestocking.

"Take mine; she is all too willing to marry," shouted another.

"Nah, begone. Your sister is still in the schoolroom," Dobberham objected.

"I have a cousin who might be available," someone else called from across the room. "Can I introduce you to her?"

Suggestions came hailing in from all sides. England seemed to be full of sisters, spinsters and single women desperate to find husbands, with their brothers all too eager to get rid of them.

Edmund knew where this was going. Once word got out that he was looking for a wife, he would be hunted down mercilessly. They would run down his doors. They would accost him in the street. There would be chance meetings that were anything but. Women would faint at his feet, stop his curricle in the park, pursue him in the ballrooms, hound him in the salons and at the opera. The time when he could sit quietly in his box would come to an end. He'd seen it happen to his friend Victor, who hadn't lasted a day under the barrage of matchmakers. He'd been dragged to the altar within a fortnight and was now living in the country with his wife, who was pregnant with their third child.

The last time he'd seen Victor, he'd seemed content, admittedly, but he'd grown a belly and whiskers, and was wearing a wrinkled coat that was hopelessly out of fashion; his sleeves decorated with stains of curdled milk and other ghastly substances he'd rather not know about.

He would not make the same mistake.

Dunstan's invitation to his country house party was the last straw. "Louise can no doubt set you up with someone," he'd said. "She insists that you come to our house party next week. She'll be so pleased!"

Edmund shuddered. Lady Louise Dobberham's notorious house parties left everyone so compromised that they were forced to marry. In fact, the lady was known to be so ambitious that she wouldn't rest until all her guests were married by the end of the event. Including the old maids and chaperones. Once, she'd locked Lord Emris and Miss Elliot, a spinster, in the library for an entire night. The next morning, they'd emerged rumpled and blushing. Emris had left immediately to obtain a special licence. To this day, Louise was proud of this achievement, for both had had the reputation of being unmarriageable. Now Edmund was constantly in Louise's sights, for as an eligible bachelor he was one of her favourite targets.

This was Edmund's tipping point. Which is why he thought it eminently sensible to raise his hand to stop the stone before it started rolling down the hill, crushing him, before it was too late. So when Dunstan announced that there was to be another such party, and Louise expected him to attend, he'd blurted out: "But I'm already married!"

"You're not. Come to our party and let Louise help you find someone."

"I tell you, it is unnecessary. The deed is already done. I've already tied the knot."

"Balderdash," Dobberham stated. "Since when? Where? How? Who is she? I haven't seen you with a woman for months. By Jove." Dobberham opened his eyes in horror. "You haven't married your Covent Garden doxy?"

"Hetty? No." He hadn't seen Hetty for over a year. She was fine and pretty and everything a doxy should be, but marry her? Edmund shuddered. Not in his wildest dreams.

"It would be just like you to do something like that," Dunstan muttered. "To get back at your family or some such nonsense. But even you wouldn't stoop that low."

Now there was an idea. Edmund thought about it for a moment. If he did what Dobberham said and married Hetty to spite his family, it would be a rich joke indeed. Then he shook his head. Dobberham was right, even he wouldn't go that far. Much as he liked Hetty, he couldn't stand her constant inane chatter, for all she cared about were bonnets. And she really had no table manners at all, the way she ate, with her mouth open and her elbows on the table.

No, he'd need someone with a bit more breeding, a bit more refinement. Someone with a bit more intellect than Hetty. Not that he himself had too much in his noodle, but it wouldn't hurt if at least his wife had some brains. Not a bluestocking, mind you, but someone who had a little more of what he lacked, which was common sense.

"Did you hear that?" Before Edmund could stop him, Dobberham rose to announce the latest news to all and sundry. "Tewkbury has married."

As soon as the words were out of his mouth, there was silence.

He must have said it with such convincing confidence, for they all believed him.

"Wot? Tewkbury got married? When did that happen?"

"Poppycock!"

"You're roasting us!"

"Lost my bet with Monmouth," groaned another. "Placed a wager you'd never marry. Not you!"

"But damn you, Tewkbury. You're shockingly negligent. You never introduced us to your wife, did you?" Rutherford wiped his forehead with a cloth and tossed it aside.

"She is a very private person, and we both prefer to

13

keep it that way. With good reason, it seems, since you are making such a drama of it."

"Wait. Is she the lady I saw with you at the opera the other night?" asked Viscount Enningford.

Edmund had gone to the opera alone, but he would not say so. He did not answer, which Enningford took as an affirmative. Edmund finished buttoning his coat, took his cane and, rather pleased with himself at having fooled everyone, took his hat.

The grapevine would do the rest.

Once word got out that he was no longer a bachelor, the matrons, mamas, matriarchs, ladies, and debutantes of the *ton* would take him off the marriage list, and that would be a good thing.

Then he could spend the rest of the Season pursuing his own interests without anyone pestering him.

"So tell me, who is it?" Dunstan pressed. They'd left the club and were on their way to Boodles.

"Er, I say." Edmund was terribly short on names. "A lady."

"A lady," Dobberham repeated. "Really." He crossed his arms. "Doing it too brown, my friend. Why this reluctance to share this vital piece of information with me? I thought we were best friends," he added in a hurt tone.

Indeed they were. They had grown up together. After Edmund had broken with everyone from his old life, his parents, his siblings, even his twin, Dobberham had been incomprehensibly stubborn in his insistence on remaining his friend. He'd followed him to London, introduced him to the clubs, the tailors and the snuff makers. He'd even introduced him to Hetty. Dobberham was probably the only person who'd ever accepted him for who he really was. So Edmund felt a pang of guilt at lying to his best and only friend.

He patted Dobberham on the shoulder. "I say, old friend, prudence! Prudence is the better part of value."

"I think you mean 'prudence is the better part of valour'—which makes no sense at all in this context. I dare say you meant to say 'patience is a virtue' or some such drivel."

"I say it is. You took the words right out of my mouth. 'Patience is a virtue,' so there." Edmund looked at Dobberham almost fondly. Yes, that was why they were friends. Dobberham understood him and didn't mind when he talked rubbish.

"You'll meet her in time." Edmund thoughtlessly rode deeper and deeper into his lies. "We were only married yesterday and not even my family knows. Not that they want to know. I mean, it's not like we're on speaking terms. Give us some room to breathe, old man."

"Yesterday!" Dobberham looked at him, thunderstruck.

Yesterday, Edmund had spent the entire morning in Jermyn Street mixing perfumes, but no one, not even Dobberham, needed to know, for he kept that part of his life a secret from everyone. "Yes, yesterday. At St George's. Father, er, James? Jones? Jacques? Whatever his name. You can check the register if you like." He waved his hand, knowing Dobberham would never do that.

He was right. "No, no, I believe you, old man, I believe you. But yesterday? Zounds." He wiped his brow with his handkerchief. "How long have you been planning to marry? How long have you been engaged?"

"It was rather hasty," Edmund began, painstakingly polishing his quizzing glass with his perfumed silk handkerchief. "It wasn't planned, I admit. But that's what love does to one, you know."

"Love." Dunstan gaped again. "Never tell me you're in love."

"Of course! Love." Edmund nodded earnestly. "'She floats with beauty through the day on the clouds with daffodils'—and all that. I say, you get my meaning."

Dobberham snorted. "If anyone can corrupt Byron and Wordsworth and smash their poetry together in one hideous quote, it's you, no doubt. But you know you don't have to play the fool when you're with me."

Edmund placed a manicured hand over his heart. "Cupid's bow pierced both our hearts and we could no longer contain our passion. We had to get married. It was urgent." Let him do what he wanted with that. Edmund stifled a grin.

"A love match! That's preposterous." Dobberham's eyes almost popped out of his face.

"Yes, passionately so. So you see, there is no need for me to attend your house party at all, for I am already firmly and irrevocably leg-shackled. I am no longer available for your lovely wife's matchmaking experiments. Alas."

Dunstan looked hurt and drew his hand to his balding head. "Louise won't be pleased," he murmured. "She won't be pleased at all, because she was most insistent on pairing you up with—never mind, never mind. It will upset all her plans. It's the way it is. It can't be helped, and if you've made yourself a tenant for life, I suppose congratulations are in order." He patted Edmund's arm tentatively.

"Thank you." Edmund coughed. "Tell Louise I'm afraid

I'll have to pass this time, because you know, so newly married and so in love, it wouldn't be right to leave one's wife so soon after the knot is tied." Edmund felt himself relax. What a wonderful idea to put everything on his fictitious wife's shoulders.

But Dunstan frowned. "Old chap, Louise will have my head if you don't come. I don't dare think of the consequences." Then his face brightened. "A-ha! I have it! You will come together, of course! You must bring your wife. Why didn't I think of that before? It's just the thing. Introduce your wife to society at Louise's party. She will love it." He rubbed his hands. "Anyway, it's boring for everyone to be single. A married couple or two might mix things up."

Edmund stifled a groan.

"But like I said..."

"Nonsense. Spend your honeymoon with us at Dunworthy House! You'll have plenty of privacy; we'll give you an entire floor, the house is big enough. And Louise will have the party, and you will come, and you will bring your wife. Party saved. Wife's wrath averted. Mine, that is. And you can introduce yours to everyone else." He waved away any protests and raised his stick. "I'll have to tell the others at the club. They'll think I'm trying to run a rig on them. You scoundrel. Keeping your marriage a secret like that!"

EDMUND CURSED UNDER HIS BREATH. CONFOUND IT! NOW how was he to summon a woman out of thin air? He couldn't just pull her out of a hat. Nor would she materialise out of his head. How he wished it were possible!

Edmund sighed as he walked down the street. Surely there were plenty of damsels who would not mind being his wife. The nuts and bolts in his brains might work backwards sometimes, but all in all, he was a desirable bachelor, with a title and a fortune to offer. And—he flicked away a speck of dust on his sleeve—he wasn't half bad to look at. He prided himself on being an Exquisite, a Beau, a Pink of the *ton*.

Thing was, he didn't want any of those damsels. None of those milk and water misses, pale and lisping and forevermore blushing. He did not want those thin, willowy figures with pale-blonde ringlets. They were all the same: colourless and dull.

No, the woman of his dreams was entirely different.

A fiery redhead would be good, he thought. With some meat on her bones and a few curves in the right places. A real woman, down to earth, practical. Someone who could hold her own.

Women like that did not exist outside his overheated imagination, he knew.

So what was he to do?

He would have to ask Hetty. Offer her a small fortune to pretend to be his wife for a fortnight only. He grimaced.

Edmund arrived home and threw his hat and stick at Jenkins, who seemed tense.

"There's a lady waiting in the drawing room," Jenkins said. "In addition to a..."

Edmund interrupted. "A lady? What lady?"

Jenkins gestured at the drawing room. "See for yourself, my lord."

Edmund stepped across the threshold and stopped.

He blinked.

A red-haired beauty lay asleep on the sofa.

A luscious creature with the most gorgeous red hair he'd ever seen. The midday sun streamed through the window, setting her hair aflame.

His jaw must have dropped slightly.

Athena. No, t'other one. Aphroditto. Whatever.

The woman of his dreams.

Just like that. Materialised.

CHAPTER THREE

*E**arlier.*

"Hanover Square Eleven." Ellen frowned at the slip of paper in her hand and glanced down at Noni. He'd slept for most of the journey and now seemed weepy, hungry, and out of sorts, as children tend to be when they've travelled too long. She'd fed him an apple, a slice of bread, and a bit of cheese, and let him finish the milk in the flask she'd brought.

The child hadn't spoken a word during the entire journey. He'd clung to her, though, with a mute question in his beautiful dark eyes. Ellen's heart clenched with compassion. The child must be frightened and confused, being dragged from one place to another. Who knew where he'd come from and what he'd been through before being unceremoniously dumped on the steps of Miss Hilversham's seminary. She ran her other hand through his thick, black hair. She wondered what had happened to his mother. He was probably an orphan, poor child. But sweet as the boy was, he wasn't really her problem. The sooner she left him in the hands of his guardian, the better.

Ellen would still have time to visit her family before catching the coach back to Bath. She hadn't seen them for over a year. Her step siblings, Jimmy and Melly, were nearly five. Their mother Jenny had given birth to another baby two months ago. She would like to greet the newest addition to the family before returning to Bath. Then there was the eldest, Drake, who was an offspring of her stepfather, Jacob Robinson's previous marriage. Ellen frowned. Jenny had written about him in her letter, greatly worried, as it seemed he'd abandoned his studies and fallen in with an unsavoury group of men whose primary pastime was gambling and drinking. It was worrying indeed.

But first: Lord Twinsbury of Hanover Square Eleven. She clamped the paper between her lips, and keeping hold of the child's hand, his trunk in her other hand, she climbed the stairs to an intimidating white terraced town-house, with an iron-railed fence and a porticoed entrance with a gleaming blue lacquered door. There was no doubt: Noni's guardian must be quite plump in the pockets if he could afford a house like this.

Ellen's hand hesitated for a moment at the brass knocker. Then she rapped sharply three times.

The door opened almost immediately, and an elderly butler peered at her suspiciously.

She still had the paper between her lips. Ellen dropped

the trunk and removed the paper from her mouth. "Is this Lord Twiksbury's residence?"

The butler's eyes wandered down her wrinkled and mud-spattered dress, spotted the child hiding behind her and raised an eyebrow. "Tewkbury is our name."

Goodness, why must butlers always be so lofty? Ellen had no great love for the aristocracy, especially when they dropped off their little charges like bundles of rags in front of the school and had arrogant butlers as gate-keepers who patronised their visitors.

She lifted her nose, narrowing her eyes to slits. "Then tell his Lordship *Tewkbury* that Miss Ellen Robinson from the Seminary of Young Ladies in Bath is here to deliver his ward." She pushed Noni forward.

The second eyebrow rose and disappeared into the man's reclining hairline.

"I wasn't aware his lordship had a ward."

"Well, he does now."

The butler looked down at Noni as if he were a stray animal. "His Lordship's not in."

"They never are," Ellen muttered. She was tired, dusty, and hungry and had no patience for it. If the butler believed he had to be patronising, then she would show him just how patronising a schoolmistress could be, which would make even the most hardened soldier tremble in his boots. All one had to do was pretend they were one of her disobedient pupils. It worked every time.

"What is your name, pray?"

"Jenkins."

"Jenkins. I shall say this only once, so listen closely. Given these circumstances, we can do one of two things. One:

leave the poor child out here in the cold rain, which will, no doubt, provoke him to throw a tantrum in the middle of the street causing him to attract all sorts of unwanted attention, not to mention the possibility of contracting a severe chill which might lead to his death, for which you will be held solely responsible. Or Two: invite us in and offer us some tea in the drawing room while we await his lordship's return." Noni would never throw a tantrum; he was too good a child. But situations like this called for desperate lies.

A look of uncertainty crossed the butler's face before it was replaced by a frown. He glanced at the child, as if pondering on Ellen's ominous ramifications, and decided with a visible shudder that it was better to let them in before the child, indeed, dissolved into a tantrum.

"You may await his lordship in the drawing room." The sour face with which he'd uttered the words made him look as if he'd licked a lemon.

"Good decision. That wasn't so difficult, now, was it?" Nose in the air, Ellen led Noni past him, leaving the trunk outside for the butler to carry in.

There was no denying it, this townhouse was all the crack. The entrance alone was a bright, airy place, with white marble floors, white panelled walls, arched porticoes above the doors, and mirrors and gilded tables along the sides. There was even a fireplace, and at the end of the hall, an elegant staircase wound its way up to the second floor.

Ellen had to admit that for a hallway, whose mundane purpose was to connect rooms, it looked like a slice of a lavish ballroom, topped with cream and frosting. The drawing room was the first room on the right with a double door, and Ellen almost sighed when she saw it. It was a large room in sage green, with full-height sash windows that looked out onto the verdant trees in the park. A white marble fireplace stood in the centre, above which was a massive painting of a landscape. Delicately upholstered, gilded armchairs in striped gold and green satin matched the wallpaper. The plasterwork on the ceiling was tasteful and classical. Mahogany tables, chests of drawers, and chairs completed the room.

Flowers sprouted from vases in every corner. The mantelpiece was decorated with pink peonies and ferns, and a matching arrangement was placed in a Greek vase on a side table.

"My goodness. How pretty." The words escaped Ellen.

Noni seemed to like the room too, for he let go of her skirt and bounced on the sofa.

Ellen's mood improved as she studied the paintings on the wall. Was that a Turner? The one on the other side of the wall was definitely a Tiverton, for she recognised the painting by her former colleague's husband at once. Whoever lived here had exquisite taste in art and decor, and that was a good sign.

She sat down next to Noni on the sofa to await his lordship's arrival.

The butler had brought in a tray of tea and a plate with tiny, triangular cucumber sandwiches. Noni devoured the entire plate on his own, and Ellen requested the butler to bring more. After he had done so with a grudging, frosty demeanour, Ellen sat back contentedly.

The clock ticked on the mantelpiece, and the sun streamed through the windows. The fire crackled in the fireplace and Noni's head fell on her shoulder. She blinked sleepily, nodded, opened her eyes again and dropped into a sleep of exhaustion.

Ellen dreamed about the seminary and how she'd overslept and was late for class. She climbed and climbed the stairs, which suddenly changed from the school's simple oak staircase to the white elegance of the Tewkbury townhouse. Would she never arrive? She was late and lost. She kept climbing the never-ending stairs. Miss Hilversham would be so disappointed in her. She needed her. She was counting on her. She expected her to take over the school one day. How could she tell her she did not want to? The thought startled Ellen, even in her dreams. *What do you mean, you don't want to stay at the school?* It was Miss Hilversham's voice, but it was also her own thoughts that echoed.

"I don't want to stay," Ellen whimpered.

"In that case, shall I call a hackney?" A voice said far away.

She opened her eyes.

This wasn't the seminary.

It was a beautiful room in green with pink peonies everywhere. Everything came rushing back to her.

The child beside her was gone.

She shot up from the sofa and looked around wildly. "Noni!"

Behind the other end of the sofa, she saw a bundle of black curls. The boy was hiding behind it.

"Oh, Noni, come here. I'm sorry I fell asleep. Everything will be..." Her eyes fell on the door.

Her jaw dropped.

For the vision that stood there was beyond anything she'd ever seen in her entire life.

The creature appeared to be a man.

What robbed her of every word was the way he looked.

He wore a pink and yellow brocade waistcoat with elaborate buttons and a deep purple coat over it. The waist looked pinched, as though he were wearing a corset, while the shoulders were wide, almost as if padded. The edges of his shirt were so high that they poked into his cheeks, and his hair towered so high on his head that Ellen wondered if it was a wig. His trousers were so tight you could see his thigh muscles straining against them. Unless that, too, was padding.

He wore paint. The cheeks were white, the lips red. And unless she was mistaken, there was a line of kohl under his eyes.

It occurred to Ellen that she was staring.

At about the same time, she realised he was staring back at her very similarly through his raised quizzing glass.

Ellen snapped her mouth shut. "Well. That was unanticipated."

He did not answer but continued to look silently at her travel-worn clothes, her threadbare pelisse and mudsplattered boots, as if she were a dirty stain on his exquisite silken Persian carpet. His nose wrinkled as if he smelled something malodorous.

A hot rush ran down her neck.

He raised an eyebrow.

His gaze continued down her dress and froze.

"I say. What, by the beard of Zeus, is this?" His voice was laced with such horror that Ellen instinctively turned.

But apart from the green brocade curtain and a celadon vase on the side table, there was nothing.

Confused, she turned back, only to see him pointing his white, manicured fingers at her.

No, not at her.

At Noni.

He'd emerged from behind the sofa and was hiding behind her, his face buried in her skirts.

Ellen took him gently by the shoulders and pushed him forward. "This is Noni. Your ward."

He took a step back in his diamond buckled shoes.

In a daze, Ellen took in that his stockings matched the colour and pattern of his waistcoat: a striped pink-yellow.

"Jenkins," the creature complained, pulling out a handkerchief and holding it to his nose, "explain the meaning of this."

Ellen stiffened. The man was not only being insufferably rude; he was showing a shocking lack of feeling for his ward.

"This is Miss Ellen Robinson, and this child is called Noni, my lord. Miss Robinson is a schoolmistress from the Seminary for Young Ladies in Bath."

He dropped the handkerchief. "A schoolmistress?" A look of antipathy flashed across his face. His kohl-rimmed eyes narrowed.

Ellen lifted her chin. "Precisely. I am an instructress. And this, as we have noted twice already, is Noni, your ward. I have returned him to you because we cannot possibly keep him at the seminary. What he needs is not a school for young women, but a..." Mother, she was about to say, but bit her lip just in time. "He, er, needs special care in a nursery, because he is too young, and he is a boy."

"I don't understand," Tewkbury complained.

Ellen sighed. Was he really as stupid as he looked? "Noni, would you like to greet your guardian?" She bent down to the boy, but he continued to hide his face in her skirts, shaking his head emphatically.

"But, my dear, you seem to suffer from a misunderstanding. As far as I know, I am not a guardian." He turned to Jenkins. "Am I?"

"I couldn't say for sure, sir. If you are, you have not informed me of it. Unless you have agreed to some sort of guardianship under special circumstances."

"Special circumstances." His lordship frowned. His quizzing glass dropped from his hand. "A terrible thought assails me, Jenkins. Did I, could I, would I have agreed to it while I was in my cups? Or rather, a wager? From the depths of my consciousness, I seem to recall a wager with Witherington. Which I may have lost."

"That cannot be ruled out, my lord."

Ellen had her own theory. Noni might very well be his natural child. That would explain the look of horror on his face upon realising he hadn't been able to get rid of the fruit of his indiscretion as easily as he'd hoped. It was the most likely and most despicable explanation.

Her lips pressed to a tight line and her hand closed protectively around Noni's.

The two men stared at Noni.

Ellen pulled out the letter. "I have got proof. It clearly says Baron Tewkbury of Hanover Square Eleven." She held it out to the baron, but he stared at it as if she'd held out a furry creature with sharp teeth.

Jenkins stepped forward, took the letter, unfolded it, and read it. "It appears to be true, sir. It asks for admission to the seminary and is signed with your name. My guess is that your last secretary, Roberts, arranged for this before he retired. I recall you telling him to deal with any last-minute business before he left, and not to bother you with any of it, no matter how urgent."

Tewkbury rubbed his temples with a groan. "That must be it. Roberts must have arranged it. I recall having been in a hurry to sign a pile of papers. That cursed wager! Jenkins, remind me not to imbibe again."

"Yes, sir. For how long?"

Tewkbury thought. "Five hours. I have to be at the club by mid-afternoon at the latest."

"Very well, sir."

"Well?" Ellen tapped her muddy boot impatiently on the carpet. It had been a long journey. She was tired and hungry and anxious to get home to her family and then back to Bath. The child would stay with his guardian, and she hoped he'd be well looked after.

She tried to gently untangle Noni's fingers out of her skirt and pushed him forward. "Why don't you go to your Uncle..." She looked at the Baron questioningly. When he didn't answer, she added, "What's your name?"

"Tewkbury."

"I know that," Ellen said with exaggerated patience. "But is that what you want a little child to call you? What is your given name?"

"Edmund Arthur."

She turned back to Noni. "Why don't you go over to your Uncle Ned and shake his hand?"

"Uncle Ned?" Tewkbury spluttered.

Noni had popped three of his fingers into his mouth and sucked on them while regarding Tewkbury's colourful glamour with amazed, rounded eyes. To Ellen's surprise, he didn't hide behind her back but did indeed step forward, taking his fingers out of his mouth and holding his hand out to Tewkbury.

Tewkbury pressed his own hand to his chest, looking panicked. His nostrils twitched.

The look Ellen shot at him would have killed the most hardened hussar.

In the slowest possible motion, Tewkbury extended two fingers and shook the boy's grubby, saliva-coated hand. Then he withdrew, wiped his fingers on his handkerchief, and handed it with two fingers to Jenkins.

Ellen rolled her eyes. This man, this fop, who looked like something out of a Cruikshank's cartoon, was not worth her time. She dropped to one knee and put her hands on Noni's shoulders. "You will stay with your guardian now." She swallowed. "He will take good care of you and show you to your own room where you will be given a lovely bath, a glass of warm milk and a good hot meal. A healthy stew with bread would be best," she added, looking hard at Tewkbury. "And then the cook will give you a biscuit—plain shortbread, not too sugary, though he is allowed a dollop of raspberry jam on it. Then you'll wash your face, brush your teeth, go to bed, say your prayers and sleep. If you ask nicely, your Uncle Ned might read you a story beforehand."

The look of utter horror on his lordship's face was so comical that she bit the inside of her cheek to keep from bursting out laughing.

She planted a kiss on Noni's forehead and stood up.

"Well then, sir. My work is done. I shall leave Noni in your good, capable hands and trust that he will be taken care of." She picked up her reticule from the sofa and started for the door. But the man was standing there, not moving. She stopped short in front of him and tilted her head aside in a question.

"Jenkins, do as she says, in exactly that order and detail, excluding my involvement in any of it. Show the boy to his room, if you please." He hesitated for a tiny moment before adding, "And also for Miss—" he looked to the butler for help.

"Robinson," he put in.

"A room for Miss Robinson too."

Ellen's head snapped up. "I beg your pardon?"

Tewkbury tapped his quizzing glass thoughtfully against his lips. "Yes." He turned to Jenkins with renewed determination. "Miss Robinson needs a room as well."

"Very well, sir." Jenkins left.

"I don't need a room. I need another cup of tea, perhaps, and something more substantial to eat, and then I need to visit my family and return to Bath."

"You may visit your family."

"How very magnanimous of you," she said sarcastically and stepped forward in another attempt to leave. But he refused to move as much as an inch. She was so close to him, she could smell him. It was astonishingly—nice. A whiff of a decent, musky perfume, mixed with pine and something masculine. Her nostrils twitched, and she had to keep herself from bending forward and sniffing him all over.

"And I daresay one can do something about tea and a morsel to eat as well."

He was taller than her, by at least half a head. His eyes were deep and dark, looking down at her in a puzzled manner. Ellen shook herself. It was merely that kohl liner.

He lifted his hand. "And then you may go to your room."

Ellen shook her head. "I am not staying here."

"Oh yes, you are," he said matter-of-factly. "For who will take care of the child if not you?"

Ellen was flustered. "I don't know. Hire a nurse, maybe?"

"Can't you be that nurse?"

Ellen looked affronted. "I am a teacher, not a nursemaid."

"Are you, now?" Tewkbury looked thoughtful.

Noni, bored by the adults' discussion, had stepped toward the side table and started playing with the porcelain rider on it.

"So I am to hire a nursemaid?"

"Indeed, that would be the best."

"What else does he need?"

Ellen stared. He was asking her? Very well. "A governess. Later, a tutor. A school room. A solid routine and wholesome food. Daily walks in the fresh air and contact with children of his own age." She took a big breath and delivered Miss Hilversham's message. "But what he really needs is a mother."

Tewkbury's quizzing glass fell.

"You are not, by any chance, married, are you, my lord?"

"I am not!" he forcefully uttered.

Ellen sighed. "I was afraid of that. It would have made things somewhat easier. Make sure to get him a governess, then."

Tewkbury groped for his quizzing glass. "Will you take the position?"

"Certainly not!"

"Why not?"

"Why not?" she echoed dumbly. Stay here as the child's nursemaid and governess? Wasn't it as plain as daylight why that would not work? "I can't possibly leave Miss Hilversham's employ."

Miss Hilversham needed her. Topic closed.

"Why ever not? I'll offer you thrice the salary you get paid at your current position."

Ellen's jaw dropped. "Thrice?"

The cogs in her mind went round and round. With that amount of money, she could quit working for several years.

She could help support her family.

Pay the children's school tuition. Help pay back Drake's debts, which Jenny said were considerable.

"For how long?"

"Indefinitely."

"It would be like a betrayal. Miss Hilversham depends on me." Ellen wrung her hands. "She wants me to take over the school." Ellen shook her head. "I can't possibly desert her like that."

"Four times the salary then, to assuage your guilty conscience?"

"Four!"

"Make it five."

She merely gaped.

"My dear girl," Tewkbury yawned, "make up your mind. The issue is quite simple, really."

"Is it?"

"Do you enjoy working there? At that—whatever place." He waved his quizzing glass around.

"Miss Hilversham's Seminary for Young Ladies isn't just any place. It's the best school in the entire kingdom. And of course I enjoy working there." Except she'd been exhausted of teaching lately. Of marking the mountain of papers that never seemed to end. Of dealing with spoiled, snobbish girls who were half adults, half children, who weren't interested in real learning but only in hauling in a husband, who had to be handled with satin gloves so that their equally spoiled parents wouldn't take them out of school; of teaching etiquette and embroidery and all the boring things when she'd rather teach literature and philosophy and visit art galleries. Miss Hilversham wanted her to be the next headmistress. But did she, herself, want that?

"Did you say five times my present salary?" It was a fortune. "You would pay so much for the child's governess?"

His lordship's sleepy eyes popped open. "Oh no. Not as his governess."

Ellen massaged her temples. "No? Then as what? As an overpaid nurse?"

"It would be as my wife, of course," he replied softly. "You did say he needed a mother."

CHAPTER FOUR

"e is mad, I tell you. Mad! Utterly, completely unhinged." Ellen sat in her family's parlour room and stirred her teacup so violently that half the contents spilled onto the saucer.

"And you left the child with a madman?" Mrs Jenny Robinson, fondly called "Stepmother" by Ellen, was a lively young woman, not much older than Ellen, with curly brown hair. She was not really Ellen's stepmother, but Ellen loved her as dearly as if she had been. Jenny cradled her newborn in her arms and bent forward, eagerly listening to Ellen's latest, incredible tale.

After his lordship's indecent proposal, Ellen had bolted from the townhouse and gone straight to her family's home in Cheapside. Jenny had been astonished to find Ellen—who never lost her composure—distraught and exhausted.

"First, we will have some tea. Then you'll tell me all about it," Jenny had said after they'd embraced.

Ellen put down the cup with a sigh. "I shouldn't have

left, should I? I should have stayed at least a night or two to see how Noni was settling in. What if he sends him away again, this time to an institution that doesn't care about children as much as we do?"

"I would say it is possible, indeed. But that proposition of his is most interesting." Jenny looked pensive. "What were his conditions?"

"I must confess, I did not stay long enough to hear them."

Jenny took a thoughtful sip from her cup. "Because he may not have meant a proper marriage at all. It's not the first time I've heard such proposals." Before she'd married Jacob Robinson, who was a widower, Jenny had been a seamstress, sewing beautiful confections for princesses, duchesses, and marchionesses. The stories she'd collected during that time could have filled a book, which would explain why she wasn't at all shocked by Ellen's horrified revelation that she'd just received a most indecent proposal from an Exquisite.

"What, to buy wives?"

"Yes. The whole aristocratic marriage mart is, as the name suggests, a marketplace where they buy and sell young women to the highest bidder. When it comes down to it, it's just a business transaction. Love has nothing to do with it. Sounds like your baron is desperate to fill the position, and now that he has a child, it would make sense that he would need a wife. You happened to be there. So he made an offer."

"He's not 'my' baron!" Ellen exclaimed.

"Well, consider it. The question is whether he needs a fake wife or a real one. Either way, for a man who does not want to settle down, hiring a wife to play the part is not such a mad idea. Though why a lord would ask a schoolmistress is, of course, the question. On the other hand, it would make sense for the good of the child. This way, he gets wife and governess rolled up in one. Saves him the expense of a governess."

Ellen groaned. "You should have seen the man! In fact, you could hardly see him. The man was somewhere underneath all that silk and paint, and I dare say he even wore a wig. That hair can't have been natural."

Jenny nodded. "He's a Tulip. One of those Bond Street Beaus. They take fashion very seriously. Some of them know more about fashion than the ladies."

"What a ridiculous race of men. I shall never understand them." Ellen shook herself. "But let's put all that aside for now." She looked around. "It's been so long. It's so good to be home. Nothing has changed. How are you all?"

The fire was crackling cosily in the fireplace, and Jenny was rocking back and forth in her rocking chair with the baby in her arms. Jimmy and Melly, the two little ones, were playing quietly on the floor. Ellen looked at them fondly.

Even though she called them family, Ellen was not related to any of them.

Jacob Robinson, who had taken her in as his daughter after her own father's death, was not really her 'stepfather', but somehow it was an apt description of their relationship, which was one of affection and respect. Ellen could not remember ever having loved her biological parents as much as she loved Jacob and Jenny.

Jacob was a brilliant scholar and writer. He spent most of his days teaching and writing his literary treatises. He had recently achieved a modest kind of fame and was invited to the literary salons of the upper classes, but that didn't mean he was making any money. So when Ellen turned eighteen, she became a schoolmistress to help support the growing family. It was Jacob who had found the advertisement in The Times. She'd applied to Miss Hilversham's Seminary, and the headmistress, stern as she looked but kind-hearted underneath, had hired her immediately.

"And Drake?" Drake was Jacob's son from his first marriage and their only cloud of worry.

Jenny sighed. "Drake. They expelled him from Cambridge. Not even Jacob's status as a scholar influenced the decision."

Ellen sat up. "Oh, no! What happened?"

"I don't know the details. He was caught drunk on the premises and offended the Dean badly. Something to do with his wife, who, it turns out, he'd fallen in love with." Jenny covered her eyes with her hands.

Ellen groaned. "Of all the impossible things!"

"Don't ask. It is beyond words." Jenny placed the baby in the cradle. She smoothed and re-smoothed the paisley patterned blanket on her lap. "But that's not the worst of it. Jacob says he's seen Drake several times since."

Ellen leaned forward. "And?"

"Drake keeps asking him for money. He's gambled away all his savings. He says he's on the run from the law and that he'll be thrown into Marshalsea if he doesn't pay up."

"Oh no!"

Jenny looked at her unhappily. "It broke his heart, but Jacob had to say no. With the new baby and schooling for the little ones, we need to find a bigger house to live in. But rent is so expensive in London. Jacob was promised a bonus payment from the lectures he gives at the Royal Institution, but we haven't seen a penny yet. The truth is, we can't afford to pay Drake's debts. We just can't. There was a fight. They parted badly. We haven't heard from Drake since. He could be in jail by now, who knows?"

Ellen sighed. "And Jacob? How is he taking it?"

"You know how he is. Stoic. But beneath his brave exterior, his heart is breaking. He has been working very hard, though, and we have seen little of him. I'll take up sewing again. It's the only way."

Ellen clasped Jenny's hands. "You are so brave and strong."

"Hush. Listen to me complain. I am otherwise happy with my life, you know?" She patted the edge of the cradle. "We're all healthy, and our home is warm and clean. I could not be happier. This is better than sitting in a small attic with ten other seamstresses, sewing lace in a poor light. I consider myself very lucky to have escaped that drudgery when I married Jacob. Now I can choose my own customers and work as much as I like. Life is so much better now, Ellen."

Jacob returned late, and a tired smile lit his face when he saw Ellen. "Ellen, my dear. What a joy to see you after all this time."

He looked older than when she'd last seen him, and his hair had turned grey at the temples, which made him look more distinguished. Ellen embraced him.

"I am afraid the news I bear regarding Drake is not good," he said over supper.

Jenny folded her arms over her chest. "Don't tell me. They finally clapped him into debtor's prison."

Jacob didn't reply, but just hunched his shoulders and sighed.

"What can we do?" Ellen looked from one to the other.

"The banks have denied me credit. Not because they mistrust me, but because they mistrust Drake. He made it into the papers this morning."

There was silence. Jenny reached out to squeeze his hand. "We will find a solution," she said. "We always do."

"We always do." Jacob nodded.

Ellen remained quiet, her head spinning.

The next morning, after she'd said goodbye to Jenny, Jacob, and the children, she stood in the street for a moment, undecided. She could go back to Bath, to Miss Hilversham, and forget this entire episode in London. Life would go on as usual, safe and sound. She could take on extra teaching hours and send whatever she could spare to Jenny and Jacob.

Or.

Or she could go back to Hanover Square Eleven.

Accept the baron's proposal.

And solve everyone's problems by pretending to be his wife.

CHAPTER FIVE

*E*dmund Graves, Baron Tewkbury, rose at his usual time the next day, which was about eleven. He had a hearty breakfast of beef and kedgeree before disappearing to his dressing rooms. He wore a banyan of bright red silk embroidered with oriental ornaments.

First, he was shaved.

As his valet sharpened the razor with a leather strop, Edmund leaned back and closed his eyes.

During this time, he liked to do something that he normally avoided during the remaining day, and that was to introspect. In other words, he pondered on the tedious business that lay ahead of him.

He needed to find a wife, urgently, since the woman yesterday had bolted after he'd suggested she marry him. Not that he could blame her; he supposed he'd sprung the proposition on her rather suddenly. But she'd left the child behind, who'd then looked up at him with bright, troubled eyes and planted his wet, sticky little hand in his. Edmund had not known what to do. So he'd told the housemaid to take the child upstairs to one of the bedrooms, and that she was to bathe him, and feed him soup with bread, followed by some biscuits.

"But only with a dollop of jam," he'd added, remembering that the woman had said the child shouldn't have too much sugar.

The child had gone willingly with the maid.

The child was one thing. He would have to deal with him later.

His lack of a wife was another.

Now that word had got out that he was supposedly married, he could no longer show his face in the clubs or on the streets until he had someone to show off.

But where would he find such a person?

Once again, he felt a pang of regret that the luscious redhead had run away. Schoolmistress or not, she'd have been perfect.

His valet, Lionel, dried his chin and flicked the towel away.

Now for the delicate business of combing his hair. His hair was thick and brown, and just the perfect length to sweep high on his forehead and back in a windswept Brutus style. He used a special pomade, mixed especially for him, to hold his hair in place.

Then he had to get dressed.

That usually took him a good two hours, sometimes three.

He had to focus his thoughts and concentrate, for it was a science.

For one did not just put on clothes.

One had to spend at least an hour carefully choosing

which apparel to wear, judging not only the quality and fabric of the coat but also the colour. This was followed by another hour of actual dressing. Sometimes it took longer because he changed his mind in the middle of the process.

And tying the cravat was another matter entirely.

Getting dressed was a sacrosanct time not to be disturbed at any cost. The butler and footmen knew better than to interrupt him, for once Edmund had dismissed a footman who'd had the audacity to announce a visitor while he was amid the delicate process of tying his cravat.

"Today," he said to Lionel, "is a green day."

"Yes, my lord. May I suggest the jade-green cloak?" Lionel held out a coat.

Edmund raised his quizzing glass to his lips and considered the green. He waved it away. "No. It's too introspective a colour. The other one."

"The hunter green?"

Edmund gave him a hostile stare. "We're not going hunting, Lionel, are we?"

"No, my lord. Certainly not." Lionel hastily tucked the offending garment away. "Er. May I ask, my lord, what you intend to do today?"

"What day is today, Lionel?" Edmund drawled.

"Wednesday."

"And what do I usually do on Wednesday?" He looked at Lionel through half-closed eyes.

Lionel blushed. He'd been his valet for almost two months now, so he should be able to rattle off his schedule without a hitch.

"After breakfast, you get dressed."

"That goes without saying," Edmund muttered, suppressing a sigh.

"Then you go to the club and fence until teatime. Then you take a walk. Then you go to the laboratory in Jermyn Street. And then to the club in St James's for dinner."

"Wrong. First, I go to the laboratory, then I go for a walk. What else?"

Lionel looked at him, taken aback. Then his eyes brightened. "And since today is Wednesday, you will go to the opera afterwards." Lionel thought a moment before adding, "You will also change clothes before the walk, the laboratory and before going to the opera."

"Indeed."

Somewhere between the club and the opera he would have to find a wife, but of course Lionel wouldn't know that.

"Very well, Lionel. Given my schedule, you can clearly see that hunter green is a poor choice for my morning visit to the club. What other greens do we have?"

Lionel scratched the back of his head. "Spinach green? Cucumber green? Parsley green?" He thought for a moment. "Mud green, moss green, mould green. What else is there? The kind of green your face gets just before you throw up your—" He caught Edmund's scathing look and interrupted himself. "I suppose not," he added hastily. "Then we have celery green, apple green and pistachio green." Lionel had reached the end of his list and was exhausted.

Edmund lifted a finger. "Pistachio it is."

"Very well, sir." Lionel went to fetch him the pistachio-green tailcoat. "May I suggest a beige striped waistcoat?"

Edmund considered the matter. "Along with the beige

46

trousers." It would be a smart ensemble. It would match perfectly. "But no. It won't do. Bring me the orange-and-yellow-striped waistcoat, the pink polka-dot waistcoat and the royal-purple waistcoat."

"Yes, sir." Lionel scrambled to get the waistcoats and laid them out.

After another half hour of trying on all three waist-coats, prancing around in front of the full-length mirror, taking them all off again, and complaining that he didn't have enough waistcoats, he settled on the orange-striped one.

The last outfit was garish, flashy, and eccentric.

A diamond brooch and fob completed the ensemble. His cravat was tied in the oriental style, and his shirt points were as high as ever.

He took a kohl stick and drew a fine black line under his lower lashes. The effect was immediate. Instead of giving him an effeminate look, it made his hazel eyes appear smoky and slightly dangerous.

"Perfect," Edmund murmured happily. His shoulders were broad, and the corset cinched his waist in just the right way. His powerful thighs needed no padding from all that fencing, and neither did his arms, but he preferred to add padding just for the fun of it.

"I need a scarlet primrose, Lionel. For my buttonhole. I shall need several of them, so that when one wilts it can be replaced with a fresh one. Can you get that, please?"

Lionel could.

Edmund had always complained that the era of maca-roni was long gone. Modern fashion was more sober, and he was bored by the simpler style in which men dressed, with the dominant colours being black, blue, brown or beige.

"Why stick to four colours when there is a whole palette of colours that the universe has given us?" he was forevermore complaining to his companions at the club. They were a group of beaus who went against the grain. The more colourful, the flashier, the brighter, the better. And Edmund was the leader of them all. Elegance was not so much his main motivation as the attention it brought. He'd flick an imaginary piece of lint from the lapel of his coat and strut down the street, nose in the air, to be admired. Baron Tewkbury certainly turned heads wherever he went, followed by whispers, giggles, and laughter.

Except, if he was really honest, it wasn't really attention that Edmund was looking for; it was something else entirely that he couldn't pinpoint. Whenever he entered a room, everyone looked at him. He would pose and smile and walk around the room, aware that all eyes were on him. He did not necessarily enjoy the moment.

But he was aware, acutely aware, that the man they were seeing at that moment, the strutting dandy, the ridiculous macaroni, was not him. And that was good. It was very, very good.

Baron Tewkbury was hiding not only from the world, but from himself. But of course, that was something he would never admit to himself.

CHAPTER SIX

*H*aving finished dressing, he minced his way down the stairs with his bejewelled cane and passed the open door of the drawing room.

He stopped. Blinked. Retracted his steps. Stared.

There was a woman on the floor. On all fours. Her rather shapely bottom turned towards him.

She raised her head, her red hair gleaming in the sunlight.

He inhaled sharply.

A small, dark-haired imp scuttled on hands and knees on the floor beside her.

"Well done, Noni. Now try to take the second thread of wool and connect the two lines, then you have a perfect 'A'. See? Well done!"

She sat up and clapped.

It was this schoolmistress who'd saddled him with the child. There had been something in her eyes that seemed to suggest she thought the boy might even be his illegitimate child. Since he couldn't be sure, he'd agreed to take the child in.

Now, thanks to her, he had a child when he needed a wife.

He'd made the offer, but she'd run away. Now she'd come back; hopefully that meant she'd changed her mind.

Which was convenient for him, but something else hit him, the implications of which hadn't sunk in until now: she was a schoolteacher.

He looked glumly at her copper-red hair, which had lost its charm in an instant.

If there was ever a race of people in this world that he detested, and there were few, for Edmund was generally a man of tolerant, genial disposition, it was most certainly schoolteachers.

They had been his bane, his nightmare, his curse.

They'd ruined his childhood.

They'd wounded his soul.

And he'd seriously considered proposing marriage to her. Scratch that, he'd already done it.

He imagined his wife being a schoolteacher.

Was he mad?

If he could ignore the fact that she belonged to that hated breed of people, she would be perfect for the position.

Her head snapped up to meet his gaze.

"You've returned." His fingers fumbled for his quizzing glass.

She flushed and scrambled to her feet. "Oh. Good morning, my lord." Her eyes grew to round saucers again as she beheld him. "Your butler said you were busy and not to be disturbed." She made a vague gesture with her hand. "I, uh, wanted to check on the child."

She was wearing a blue dress today, plain and mud-free.

The child smelled much better than yesterday, sweet and clean. Yesterday, he had smelled of sour milk, and there had been an overpowering whiff of horse manure that had enveloped both of them, as one or both of them had undoubtedly stepped into a pile. Edmund stifled a shudder.

The child jumped up, and would you know, stepped towards him with an outstretched hand. The little blighter was about to repeat the saliva-covered handshake of the day before.

Edmund took an involuntary step backwards, clasped his hands behind him and stared at the little boy as if he were a wild creature, which, of course, he was.

"Won't you say good morning?" the soft voice of the schoolteacher—dash it, what was her name again?—penetrated through his mind. She was undoubtedly talking to the boy, but the strange look in her green eyes and the barb in them seemed to indicate that she meant him.

He was instantly transported back to the schoolroom and reduced to the shy, stammering boy he once was.

"G-good morning." He hadn't stammered for two decades, and as soon as a bloody teacher showed up, it all came back? He would rip his tongue out if he could, only it wouldn't work. He'd know; he'd tried it once. All he'd ended up with was a bleeding tongue, a scolding teacher, and an even more persistent stammer.

With the child standing right in front of him, with his big, black, hopeful eyes and his chubby hand still outstretched, Edmund extended, after some considerable inner struggle, a finger or two to shake his hand, just to put an end to this ridiculous situation.

At least this time, the child's hand was not wet. It was soft and warm. He dropped it like a piece of charred ember.

"Well done, Noni. You did very well."

Illogically, he felt a rush of relief, as if she'd meant him.

Irritation flashed through him. This was exactly why he should not have any teachers under his roof. Or children. Not only were they a nuisance and an inconvenience, but they stirred in the pits of his memory like the witches of Macbeth in their cauldron. It steamed and puffed and bubbled, and all sorts of strange things came out that one would have preferred to remain in the cauldron.

He would have to put his feelings aside and concentrate on the practical.

"I say, what's this you're doing?" he drawled, trying to hide his unease.

"Since I was waiting for you, and not knowing how long you would be, I thought I would use the time to teach Noni the alphabet."

Edmund stared grimly at the letter that Noni had laid out with scarlet woollen strings. "You're teaching him with woollen strings on the floor?"

The red-haired creature nodded. "I asked the maid to bring me some wool. I hope you didn't mind that I used it for this purpose. You can also use other materials such as sticks or pieces of straw."

"Whatever happened to plain slate and chalk?" The back of his head ached just thinking about slates, as his schoolmates had thrown them at him at every opportunity.

"In my limited experience of teaching younger children, for I am a teacher of older girls, if you remember, I have learnt that the little ones retain the alphabet better if they do it this way, with their hands, before they are required to hold a real pencil or piece of chalk, which they may find difficult. Besides," she shrugged, "I don't have any chalk or slates here, do I? But that's not why I came back." She took a deep breath. "I've been thinking things over, and I want to take you up on that offer you made yesterday. Assuming it still stands."

She looked him straight in the eye. Green, they were. Like shards of emerald.

He stared at them, stunned. Then he collected himself. "It still stands."

She seemed to exhale in relief. "Well, that's good."

He rang for Susie, who took the child to the nursery.

The woman remained with him in the drawing room, fiddling with the bottom button of her spencer. It was a hideous mustard-coloured thing that clashed with her dress. First thing to do was to get a new wardrobe for her.

No, wait. The first thing was to get married.

Not even that. He was getting ahead of himself. He paced the room, trying to gather his thoughts. "The first thing is to get a special licence," he thought aloud. "Archbishop. St George's. Madame Minion." He nodded to himself. That was the right order.

"Madame Minion? Who is she?"

"A dressmaker."

She stared at him blankly.

"We're going to Dobberham's country house party

early next week, and you can't go like that." He waved his fob at her. "Madame Minion is the only one who can get you fully dressed in just three days."

She nodded reluctantly.

"And St George's for the wedding, of course," he added.

"Is that necessary if it is to be a pretend marriage to begin with?"

Edmund stared. "I say. You appear not to be caring for your reputation at all, do you?"

Her cheeks flushed rosy. "I was just thinking it is an unnecessary complication."

"It would protect you from disgrace afterwards."

She looked at him with round eyes.

He took another turn, stopped, stared out of the window and watched the sun's rays dapple between the leaves of the trees. "To be clear. It would be a marriage in name only." He turned his head to watch her answer.

"Of course. I would have expected nothing more."

Was he imagining it, or did she look relieved? For some reason, it irked him.

"You will be my wife in name, appearance and conduct —in public, that is. Are you a good actress?"

"I don't know. I suppose I could be."

"You have to be. People have to believe this is a, um, love match. In private, you can do whatever you want, provided you keep the child out of my sight."

She stared at him; eyes wide. "A love match?" She emphasised the word love.

"Yes." He watched her closely.

"Oh, dear." She rubbed her left eyebrow. "May I ask —why?"

He scowled. "Circumstances are such that, for one

reason or another, the whole *ton* believes I am married. They think it was a hasty love match, so no one was informed. No banns, or late newspaper announcements. It is not to my detriment, on the contrary. Keeps the matchmaking mamas at bay. But now I need a wife to play the part, and I have no taste for insipid, whey-faced debutantes or fortune-hunting widows. Nor do I care to waste my time in Almack's looking for someone suitable. I need someone now. Immediately." He paused for a moment, then added, "And you'll do."

"And I'll do," she echoed blankly. Then she pulled herself up, a hard glint in her eyes. "You didn't mention the love match before. That will change things a bit if I have to keep up the pretence of being, er, in love with you."

"What do you mean, change?"

"In terms of price."

"How much do you need?"

She gave him a sum. The amount was probably less than five times her salary. She didn't have a good head for business, it seemed, but then, neither did he.

"I need that amount now, immediately." She twisted the edge of her spencer in her hands, crumpling the material.

Edmund frowned. "Why that particular sum?"

She took a deep breath. "To bail my stepbrother out of jail."

His eyebrows shot up. Now they were getting to the heart of the matter. "I say. A jailbird. What's he done?"

"Don't worry, he's not a murderer or a thief or anything like that. He is a gambler." Now it was her turn to walk around the room. "Drake has fallen in with the wrong crowd. How that happened, I do not know. Instead of continuing his university studies, he must have visited the gambling hells where he lost a fortune." Ellen swallowed. "A fortune he did not have." She hung her head. "A fortune no one has, for my stepfather is unable to bail him out. Neither can I." Her eyes filled with tears. "If no one gets him out, he will probably catch some terrible infection and die. They say these prisons are terrible. And if he doesn't die, Jacob, my stepfather, will ruin himself trying to raise the money."

Edmund tapped his fob against his lips. For some reason, that little tap helped him think. If this Drake fell in with the wrong crowd, and he was the green, innocent type, it was all too easy to see how he'd been fleeced by the more hardened gamblers. He'd seen it happen time and time again, which was one reason he stayed away from the gambling hells himself.

"Here is my offer. I'll bail your brother out, and I'll even go one step further. I'll buy him a commission in the army."

"Would you really?" Tears welled up in her eyes, turning them an even brighter green.

He looked away. "And you will receive a handsome annual allowance, which will ensure that you are taken care of for the rest of your life after we have ended the charade. Annulment due to non-consummation should do the trick."

"But annulments are exceedingly difficult, if not impossible, to obtain. Are you certain this will work?"

"Then we'll come up with some other excuse. We'll say that we weren't right for each other, decide to part amicably and lead separate lives. It happens to married people all the time. I'll be left in peace, and you'll have a comfortable life and never have to work again."

"And in return, I have to pretend to be your wife and be madly in love with you. Especially at that house party." Ellen swallowed. "How long do you think we'll stay married?"

Tewkbury frowned. "As long as it takes. We may have to accept a few extra invitations, go to a ball at most, but I daresay it won't be much. West, my man of business, will draw up some paper to be signed; some sort of agreement on the, er, nature of this transaction."

That sounded awkward, but that was what it was, wasn't it? Ellen nodded. "Let's do it," she said firmly. "One more thing."

"Yes?"

She looked at him hesitantly. "I need to do some shopping for Noni. There is nothing in this house that is suitable for the child. He needs toys and school supplies."

"Yes, yes." The last thing he wanted was to be pestered with details of her lessons. "Buy whatever you need, and for heaven's sake, go to Madame Minion immediately. But don't involve me in any of this."

She pursed her lips in disapproval. "A good guardian would be interested in the welfare of his ward."

He curled his lips into a sarcastic smile. "As you have no doubt noticed, I am not a good guardian." He bowed and stepped quickly out into the foyer, lest she continue to harass him with further details of his flawed sense of responsibility.

"Very well, sir." She turned.

A whiff of something entered his nostrils. "Stop."

"Sir?"

A scent that eluded him, that he could not identify.

He closed his eyes and furrowed his brow. What was it?

He turned, stepped up to her, took her hand, twisted it, and raised it to his nose.

He heard her gasp, but he closed his eyes and concentrated on the warm, feminine scent. Myrtle, lemon blossom, coconut oil and... something else. Something floral, sweet. But fleeting.

He looked up fully into her big round eyes, her eyebrows drawn together, her head tilted in confusion, her cheeks burning scarlet.

It occurred to him he was standing with the schoolmistress in the middle of the foyer, and to any outsider it would appear that he had pressed her wrist to his mouth in a passionate, lingering kiss.

He dropped her hand as if it had burned him.

"It's nothing," he muttered and made his way out of the house.

That scent. What was it?

He could not rid himself of the smell and the feeling of tender skin on the inside of her wrist. It had been creamy and soft and silky.

He got into his carriage and thought about it the entire trip to the Doctors' Commons, the law courts south of St Paul's, to obtain the special licence.

CHAPTER SEVEN

*J*t took Ellen a good while to compose herself after the baron had left.

What on earth had that been all about?

He'd appeared out of nowhere, a garish vision of colour and elegance. Was it elegance? She wasn't even sure. He was certainly an eyeful, and one couldn't help but stare when he'd suddenly appeared. He'd seemed disapproving, and she'd felt terribly self-conscious in her old dress and worn-out boots. He had also disapproved of Noni, which she couldn't countenance.

But she'd agreed to his proposal.

They would have to pretend to be in love. Good heavens!

It was an unconventional proposal. It was thoroughly improper; but by pretending to be his wife, it eliminated the awkwardness that would have resulted if she'd stayed with Noni as a mere governess in a bachelor's household. After all, what difference would it make? They would still lead separate lives. She'd be teaching and caring for Noni, not having to worry about her reputation. As a married lady with a title, people would treat her with more respect. She'd receive sufficient funds to set aside for a stable future. Drake would be helped. It was a good thing, even a blessing. The baron's proposal had saved her entire family.

But then he'd taken her hand and sniffed at her wrist. He'd clasped it tightly, and she'd noticed that his hands were broad, and his nails were trimmed to perfect ovals, and were not at all feminine as one might expect, but graceful and strong.

A lock of brown hair had fallen across his forehead and at first she'd thought he was kissing her hand.

But no. He was sniffing it.

That had sent her into such a turmoil of conflicting emotions—flattery, surprise, embarrassment, but also something else. A strange but imperceptible tremor had shaken her. Then there had been a warm tingling in the depths of her being that had flowed through her entire body until she'd felt breathless and quite hot. She would have pulled her hand away, but he'd dropped it abruptly and walked out of the house without a second glance.

It was the strangest encounter she'd ever had with a man. Granted, she hadn't had many.

And now, she would have to write to Miss Hilversham. Ellen groaned.

How was she to explain this?

A cold stone settled in her stomach. She felt like Judas. Would Miss Hilversham ever forgive her?

She sat down at the pretty little desk and pulled out a drawer. There was paper, along with some quills and ink.

By the time she'd finished both letters, it was evening.

Her stomach made a loud, awkward sound. She put a hand over it. Noni would have been fed by now. She'd have to check on him and see if he was comfortable. Perhaps there was a way for her to find some food as well.

Ellen made her way down the stairs and passed the drawing room, which she saw was empty.

She followed the hallway, now sparkling with all the candles that had been lit—oh my, you could dance on the polished marble floor—and with a hint of exuberance, she whirled around.

A maid came out of a room and stopped when she saw Ellen.

"Your dinner is served in the dining room, miss," the maid said. "If you would follow me."

The dining room was grand, with sparkling chandeliers and a vast table set for one.

Was Ellen to dine here, all alone?

She drew a hand over her dress and frowned. She had no other dress to change into. With a pang of alarm, she wondered if the baron would dine with her.

"Perhaps it would be better if I ate in my room," she began.

"His lordship has gone to the club," the maid explained, and Ellen relaxed. She stepped to the table. The basket of fresh rolls smelled heavenly.

Her stomach rumbled, and she decided to throw all etiquette to the wind and eat, whether or not she was presentable. The hearty lamb stew that was served was simple, but divine. Ellen had never eaten so much in her life.

Returning to her room, she realised she'd have to visit the dressmaker first thing in the morning. She wasn't in the least prepared for this position. She had neither the clothes, supplies, nor books to teach Noni. Perhaps something could be done about the books. Surely the baron had them somewhere in the library. She'd just have to find the room first.

THE NEXT MORNING, A MAID HAD IRONED HER DRESS, BUT Ellen sighed when she saw her boots. With the soles on the verge of falling off, no amount of cleaning could make the worn-out pair of boots look like new. There was nothing she could do about it. She would have to wear them again until she had time to buy a new pair.

Ellen had admired the pitcher and jar on the washstand, made of Meissen porcelain, exquisitely decorated with pink and gold roses and so delicate that she hardly dared use them. Next to the washbowl, which looked like an oversized rose leaf, was a small bar of soap wrapped in silk paper. Ellen lifted it reverently to her nose and sniffed. It was Pears soap. Heavily taxed and unaffordable for most people, only the wealthiest households could afford this item of luxury.

What a lovely change from the cheaper, unscented soft soap, which they used at the seminary. After a moment's hesitation, she unwrapped the soap from the silken paper and held the translucent, oval bar in her hands. A delicate floral scent wafted into her nose. How lovely.

She washed her hands and face using the soap, and dried herself with the towel that lay next to the bowl.

Now she must find the library. Where was it? She went down to the first floor and looked in every room. Ellen entered the drawing room she'd been in yesterday, then a smaller drawing room in red next to it, and a third door revealed a drawing room in blue. All the rooms were very pretty and tastefully furnished. Another door was at the end of the hall, before the staircase that led down to the kitchen.

Just as she reached for the door, it opened, and a gentleman stepped out.

Ellen jumped.

"You must be Miss Robinson." He had a clean-shaven, pleasant face, was immaculately dressed and held several sheets in his hands. "My name is West. Robert West. I am his lordship's secretary."

"How do you do, Mr West? I apologise for wandering around at random. But I was looking for the library."

"The library?"

"Yes, I assumed that was where I would teach Noni."

Mr West looked at her with a slight frown between his eyebrows. "There is no library here, but you can modify one of the drawing rooms for your purposes."

"No library?" She gaped. Then she recalled herself. "I see. Are you saying I could take, say, the red room and turn it into a schoolroom?"

"Yes, indeed."

"But the drawing rooms are far too beautiful to be turned into schoolrooms."

"That is his lordship's instruction, Miss Robinson."

"I shall need equipment. A blackboard, chalk, paints, paper, primers, toys, a globe..."

"If you could step into my office for a moment, Miss Robinson? There are some papers I need you to sign."

She stepped into a small room, which was simply but tastefully furnished with a massive mahogany desk, a shelf filled with files from floor to ceiling, a fireplace, and two upholstered leather chairs in front of it.

"Please." Mr West motioned toward a chair.

Ellen sat.

"I conduct his lordship's business," he explained. "It may interest you to know that we have bailed your brother out of prison. Furthermore, we have purchased him a commission in the Infantry, which he has accepted. He sends his regards."

She closed her eyes in relief. "Thank you," she whispered.

"Don't thank me. It was all part of the agreement you made with his lordship, yes?" He placed a contract in front of her. "If you could sign this, please."

She scanned the document and signed. Tewkbury had already signed it, with the same illegible scrawl he'd used in Noni's letter.

"Excellent. I believe his lordship has obtained the special licence, which means you will be married this afternoon at St George's. It is an unconventional time, for marriages tend to take place in the morning; however, given the circumstances, Father Kent has agreed to marry you despite this short notice, for he is a family friend of the Tewkburys, and delighted to learn that his lordship is finally marrying."

Nervousness flooded through Ellen. "It is all rather sudden. But very well." The sooner they got this over with, the better. She was thankful that she'd remembered to take along a clean dress when she stayed at Jenny's. She was wearing it now, a simple long-sleeved brown dress with a velvet mustard-coloured spencer that Tewkbury had eyed with misgiving. This would be her wedding dress. If he did not like it, it was too bad, for she had nothing else to wear.

"The servants have been informed that they are to receive a new mistress."

This explained why Jenkins had been particularly formal towards her this morning.

Mr West pulled out a piece of paper and a pen. "Please make a list of all the necessary items for the child here."

Noni was still very young, so apart from clothes, he needed the basics of school supplies. Puzzles, *The Rudiments of Grammar in Verse*, games like dominoes, a top, spillikins, a horse stick, a rocking horse and books. She also needed a tray, sand, watercolours, paper, clay, and pencils.

"That should do for now." Ellen handed the list to Mr West, who looked through it. She walked to the door and hesitated. "Mr West. What sort of man is the baron? If I may be so bold as to ask."

Mr West leaned back in his chair and considered her question. "A fair employer. He inspires great loyalty in his staff and is generally well liked. He is not at home much, though."

"He is not?"

"He gets up rather late and spends most days and nights in the clubs."

"I see."

"If I may say so, miss." Mr West hesitated for a moment before continuing. "But I think he will make an excellent husband. Even if the marriage is only in name."

"I hope so," Ellen murmured.

WHEN ELLEN WAS YOUNGER, SHE'D BELIEVED IN TRUE LOVE. She'd been a hopeless romantic who believed she'd marry her knight in shining armour, who she'd love with all her heart and who'd love her in return. She'd dreamed of getting married in St Paul's, which would be bursting with people who'd share her happiness. And they would ride off into the sunset in an open carriage to live happily ever after.

What had come of that was a broken heart and shards of disillusion. The dewy-eyed Ellen who'd dared to dream those dreams was long gone, replaced by a practical young woman who'd proved to herself that she could very well make her way in this world alone. Without a man, without marriage, and without love.

Now, through the odd twists and turns of fate, she found herself standing at the altar of St George's marrying a man she'd never in her wildest dreams thought she'd ever wed, a most unsuitable man; a complete stranger she'd known for less than twenty-four hours.

The whole ceremony passed like a dream. She kept telling herself it was all a sham, none of it real. She half expected a bolt of lightning to strike them down as they said their vows. Vows they did not mean.

Vows that were lies.

With this ring I thee wed, with my body I thee worship, and with all my worldly goods I thee endow...

They were such beautiful words.

She lifted her eyes to meet his, and perhaps that had been a mistake, for there was a peculiar intensity in his as he took her hand and gently slipped a gold band on her finger.

She looked down at their clasped hands, something catching in her throat.

When she looked up and saw the doddering old man of a priest beaming at them, she knew the deed was done.

She was married.

CHAPTER EIGHT

*I*t was done.

He was married.

Completely out of his depth, Edmund did what he thought was the only natural thing for a newlywed husband to do: he fled.

He spent an hour or two in his laboratory mixing perfumes, but he could not find the scent which hung around her. His wife, that is. Must get used to thinking of her as such.

Thoroughly annoyed, he went to his fencing club. An hour of fencing was the thing to do, of course. But that had not been satisfying, either, since everyone kept insisting on congratulating him again, which only hammered the notion home that he was indeed firmly clapped in parson's mousetrap and there was no escape, at least for the time being.

On his way to his club, he decided, with Dobberham in tow, to get roaring drunk.

Edmund got out of the coach and, looking up the road, saw someone familiar.

A curvaceous female in a horrible mustard-yellow spencer, wearing a tattered bonnet, was about to enter a dressmaker's shop across the road.

"There she is."

"Who?" Dobberham squinted.

"My wife." Edmund went after her, not noticing that Dobberham was following him.

ELLEN HAD BEEN RELIEVED WHEN THE BARON, THAT IS, HER husband—for she ought to start thinking of him in that manner—had left right after the wedding.

There had been a tiny twinge of disappointment deep down, but she'd crushed it like an irritating bug under her heel. There was much to do, much to prepare, much to organise. It was to be a busy afternoon, as she had shopping to do for Noni and herself.

She needed clothes.

So the first thing Ellen did as the new Lady Tewkbury was to go shopping.

She set off with a maid. She needed strong, practical clothes and sturdy shoes. Before going to Bath, Ellen used to go shopping with Jenny in the linen drapers of Cheapside and Covent Garden. Jenny was good at finding a bargain. So it seemed natural for Ellen to go there and buy some sturdy dove-grey cotton, one plain and one twilled, and a few lengths of brown tweed for a warmer dress. That would do. Next she visited a boot and shoe warehouse where she bought two pairs of leather walking boots and a finer pair of slippers for more formal occasions, and for suppers in the intimidating dining room. She pulled on one pair of boots and immediately disposed of her old, worn-out pair.

Then it was on to that Mme Minion's to have her dresses made.

Mme Minion's shop was extravagant and displayed not only the latest fashions in the finest silk, satin and poplin, but also hats and gloves.

Ellen stared doubtfully at the display. It looked terribly expensive. But Tewkbury had told her to come here, so here she was.

"Let's go in, then," Ellen said to her maid as she pushed the door open. A small bell rang.

Mme Minion was a small, energetic woman with dark hair and bright eyes. "I am happy to make you any number of dresses you wish," Madame told her. "I can make you a complete wardrobe according to the latest fashion, at a very good price. But not with this material, milady. S'il vous plaît! It is hideous!" She lifted the grey fabric between two fingers and wrinkled her nose. "You can store potatoes or coal in it, but it cannot encase the delicate figure of a woman. It is sacrilege!"

"But, Madame, it is a very proper fabric, strong and practical, and eminently suitable for me."

But Madame shook her head. "No, no, no, and no! You see, the colour does not suit your complexion at all. You have a beautiful complexion, and your hair, mon dieu, take off your awful bonnet, please."

"But..."

Without much ado, Mme Minion took off her bonnet

and cast it aside. "Ah. I knew it. Look at your hair. Your glorious hair! Aphrodite would be jealous. You must wear pomona green and china blue to set off the glory of your hair. The ladies of the *ton* will rage with jealousy."

"Really?" Ellen looked astonished. "I thought red hair was horribly out of fashion."

Madame Minion tutted. "The trick, milady, is to follow fashion and then break it. You want to be an arbiter, not a slave to fashion." She turned and her face broke into a smile. "Just like milord!"

Ellen whirled around.

Tewkbury stood in the middle of the shop and smirked. Where had he sprung from? He threw her into confusion. For the last time they'd seen each other was in church, and he'd vowed to cherish and love her till death do them part. And now he was beaming at her as if she were the most precious thing in the world.

It almost made her believe she was.

Heat flooded through her body.

He bowed to Madame, who held out her hands, and he kissed the tips. "Truer words were never spoken." Then he took Ellen by the hand and drew her to him.

"Sir!" Ellen's cheeks flushed scarlet. Then she remembered herself. "I mean, Tewkbury. What a j-joy to see you. So unanticipated."

Her husband gave her a smile so brilliant and warm it took her breath away. "My love," he said huskily, planting a kiss on her hand. "It has been so long. Time passes slowly when not in your presence." He pulled her close so she could smell his cologne. "Dobberham's looking through the window," he murmured as he planted a kiss on her temple. "Spying on us. Play the part."

Oh. So he was merely playacting. Ellen glanced furtively at the window. A stout gentleman with a receding hairline was indeed peering through the glass into the shop.

"Ignore him and act naturally." He put his arm around her. "We just got married, you know," he told Madame Minion.

She clasped her hands in delight. "Oh! Congratulations! What joy! I understand now. Of course, you are looking for a new wardrobe for your lovely wife." She beamed at them.

"I say. Wanted to enquire if the new fabrics have arrived?" he asked.

"They have indeed! Everything for my favourite customer. I shall fetch them immediately. The finest silks, royal embossed satins, and a very fine bombazeen in a beautiful, rich orange. You will love it, my lord! But first, let me attend to your wife."

Edmund nodded. "It must be said that it is most urgent. We need a complete wardrobe in three days."

Madame clasped her hands over her head and proclaimed it was impossible.

After much back and forth, she conceded that there might be one or two dresses that would fit milady.

"I trust your good judgement. What would you recommend?"

"We've had a bit of a disagreement, Lady Tewkbury and I. Your wife wants that awful grey, but I won't have it." Mme Minion set her mouth in a mulish line. "It's a crime."

"The grey won't suit her," Tewkbury agreed. "Some warmer colours, though. A warmer shade of blue and green."

Madame Minion's face broke into a smile. "Just as I said." She whisked away and returned with a dress in forest green. "This one. It was ordered but never collected. It needs to be taken in at the hem, just a little, I think, and a little at the back..."

It was a silk sarsnet dress with puffed sleeves and a delicate net of embroidered flowers. The hem was trimmed with flounces.

Ellen pulled a face. She could never teach Noni in that. "It's far too green, and the material isn't right at all! I just need a plain, practical day dress."

But both Edmund and Madame Minion ignored her.

"The fabric is exquisite." Edmund fingered the material. "It flows."

"Exactly! The movement is graceful and supple."

"It skims and glides with stealth."

Ellen wrinkled her forehead. "Are we talking about the fabric or a predatory animal?"

Both heads turned to look at her. Edmund raised the cloth to her face. "Lovely," he murmured. "We'll take it. She'll need a shawl to go with it. Spencer, bonnet, slippers, gloves, reticule."

"But..."

Madame Minion beamed. "Excellent. You read my mind, as usual. She will also need at least two walking dresses, a carriage dress, a morning dress, two evening dresses and a ball gown. You are in luck. I have several such gowns that will suit her perfectly. She has a wonderful figure, does she not?"

They both eyed her figure, Madame with a calculating eye as she took measurements, and he with open appreciation.

Ellen blushed.

"She does, indeed."

"She must also try on the new silk that has just arrived. It will fit her like—" she kissed her fingers.

Ellen tried on a shocking number of dresses behind a screen, while Tewkbury flipped through the latest fashion plates from *La Belle Assemblée*, and Madame Minion danced around her, poking her with pins. She put on wraps, shawls, spencers, pelisses, redingotes, fichus. Not to mention gloves, hats, bonnets and, with a twinkle in Mme Minion's eye, a nightdress so flimsy it left nothing to the imagination.

After Mme Minion had taken her measurements and talked about various stays, undergarments and petticoats, Ellen decided that enough was enough.

"We must have a talk," she hissed to Tewkbury after Madame Minion had gone to look for some silks at the back of the shop. "This can't go on. She's putting together an enormous wardrobe for a lady."

A corner of his lip curled upwards. "I say. Aren't you a lady?"

"Of course I am. I mean, not in the way she thinks I am." She tugged at her right earlobe. "You know what I mean!" She leaned forward and whispered. "You are spending a fortune on a pretence."

Tewkbury sighed. "I refuse to be married to a woman who walks around in dull, grey clothes, looking like a schoolmistress. It depresses me. Consider all this," he raised a hand, "as part of the contract. You must look the part. Remember the house party next week? Dobberham is waiting outside like a shark. Keep the new walking dress on. It suits you to perfection."

If the baron wanted to go bankrupt, buying a new wardrobe for his new pretend wife, that was his problem, wasn't it? But look at that glorious gold ball gown with silver trimmings, roses and a gauze net! She'd never touched anything so lovely in her entire life.

"Excellent. You will be the belle of the ball, the diamond of the Season!" Madame Minion clasped her hands together. "Leave the fabric you bought here." Mme Minion took the parcel from the maid. "You will not need it. I'll make pillowcases out of it." She wrinkled her nose. "No, not even pillowcases. They will scratch your cheeks. Sacks for storing turnips."

"But..." Ellen protested. "It is good, solid fabric!"

Edmund pushed Ellen out of the shop. "Thank you, Mme Minion. It was a pleasure, as always."

"She kept my fabric!"

"So she did."

"Ah, took you ages." Dobberham pounced on them as soon as they set foot on the street. "I was about to grow roots here."

"Dobberham." Edmund took Ellen's hand in his. "Ellen, may I present my good friend, Lord Dunstan Dobberham? We are to be his guests next week."

Dobberham made a flourishing bow, then took her hand and planted a wet kiss on it. "Lady Tewkbury. So he wasn't lying, the scoundrel. And now I understand why he felt he had to hide you and marry you in secret. So you wouldn't be carried off by someone else."

"I say. Talking nonsense is my speciality," Tewkbury put in.

"Louise will be delighted to meet you."

"Louise is his wife," Tewkbury explained.

Ellen, out of her depth, smiled uneasily at him. He seemed nice enough, but she felt uncertain about how to behave like Lady Tewkbury. She was but a mere schoolmistress, after all. Not a proper lady.

CHAPTER NINE

The coach rattled through the countryside, and the child had finally fallen asleep. Edmund was trying to do the same as he leaned back with his arms crossed and his eyes closed. But sleep eluded him. She— that is, the schoolmistress who was now his wife—Ellen— must remember her name—had put the child's head on her lap and carefully spread a woollen blanket over the child's body. Very maternal behaviour, he thought, especially towards a child who wasn't hers. He knew from personal experience that not all women were so motherly, and her behaviour struck him as oddly pleasant. That, in turn, surprised him because he hadn't realised that was a trait he liked in women.

He'd watched her through half-closed lashes as she stared out of the window, chewing on her lower lip. He wondered if she regretted her marriage. He wondered what she thought of the ridiculous situation he'd put her in. He wondered what she thought of him. No, he didn't;

he'd rather not know. Not that it mattered, because it was too late for regrets now.

Odds fish, he really ought to stop thinking so much; this exertion only addled his brain.

She wasn't exactly beautiful, with her wide mouth and deep-set green eyes. There were a few freckles on her cheeks, which he found charming, but which no doubt caused her much distress, as freckles were decidedly frowned upon and out of fashion. Her most beautiful feature was her hair, which was now tied back and tucked under one of Mme Minion's bonnets. She wore a blue velvet carriage dress, with a matching pelisse and gloves, and looked all the crack.

In short, she looked like Lady Tewkbury.

He approved.

This morning he'd merely nodded at her when they'd met in the dining room for breakfast. She'd looked beautiful in her new dress, and he hadn't known what to say to her now that they were married. Anyway, there had been little time to talk as the servants had bustled about packing and stowing their trunks in the carriage.

For today, they were off to Dunworthy House.

The coach drove through rolling hills and meadows. He didn't need to open his eyes to take in the scenery; he knew it all too well. After all, he'd spent his childhood here, scrambling across the fields with Dunstan, falling out of trees and half-drowning in the nearby stream. Aye, he admitted he had some childhood memories he was fond of.

Not all had been dominated by fear.

Not everything had been struggle and strife. He sighed. Most of the time, he preferred not to think about his childhood. He hadn't in a long time, and he did not intend to begin now. Yes, he knew it well, that stretch of land they were passing through, bordering on Dobberham's estate, and seeing it caused a pain deep in his heart that he'd rather not feel. He was wise to keep his eyes tightly shut.

By the changing sound of the gravel under the wheels, Edmund could tell that they were entering the park, where the sweeping chestnut avenue led up to a sweeping Palladian mansion: Dunworthy House.

Dobberham's estate was handsome, to say the least. He liked to show off his mansion, and his wife threw the most lavish and elaborate house parties in England. There would inevitably be picnics, excursions and at least one glamorous ball, if not two.

Lady Louise Dobberham did not believe in segregating the sexes. While she allowed the men to pursue their activities of hunting, fishing and shooting in the morning, she insisted they return punctually at midday to spend the afternoon with the ladies. It was unorthodox, but she was Lady Dobberham, and it was her house party, and she could do as she pleased.

"I refuse to sit indoors on a perfectly sunny day, sewing or reading, while the men are out enjoying themselves. Besides, they have had their share of fun in the morning, doing their sports. In the afternoon, I insist they devote their time to us ladies."

As a result, Louise's parties were hugely popular.

She was known as a meddlesome matchmaker, and the whole purpose was to match up all their guests. Every minute was spent in games, activities, musicals, plays, picnics, outings and many other things that forced the men to interact with the women. It would be no different this time.

Dobberham and his wife stood at the entrance, greeting their guests.

"Tewkbury." Dobberham grinned. "You made it. And Lady Tewkbury. Welcome. My wife, Lady Louise Dobberham."

Louise was a petite lady with strawberry-blonde curls. She looked like a delicate porcelain doll that might break if she fell, but her appearance belied reality: the lady was a whirlwind of energy and as strong-willed and unbending as iron. Dunstan liked to joke that she was the real man of the house. In fact, before they'd married, she'd had a somewhat scandalous reputation for being wild and flighty, dressing in men's clothes, riding astride and smoking cigars. Dunstan had told Edmund he'd adored her from the first moment he'd set eyes on her. For some reason, she'd fallen in love with him, too. He wasn't eye candy with his paunch and balding head, so Dobberham didn't deceive himself that she married him for his looks. But perhaps his quiet, steady personality was the right anchor for her flightiness. They were an unlikely couple, but it was a love match.

Which meant that Louise, in particular, would not be easily fooled by his own supposed love match with Ellen. They would have to be very convincing.

Edmund put an arm around Ellen and smiled warmly into her eyes, causing confusion to flicker across her eyes. "My sweet, Dunstan and Louise are my closest friends. You have met Dunstan, and how happy I am that you are now to meet his wife, Louise."

Louise looked at Ellen with open curiosity and took

her hand in hers after Edmund had released it. "I cannot tell you how pleased we are to finally make your acquaintance. For the longest time, we were sure that Tewkbury had told us a terrible fib when he said he was married. I wouldn't believe Dobberham at all when he'd mentioned it. But here you are! How wonderful it is." She slipped an arm through hers and walked with her into the cool interior of the large house. "It will be such fun! I have planned a great party, which I hope will be very enjoyable for everyone."

"I'm sure we will enjoy it very much, Lady Dobberham," Ellen replied.

"Please. Call me Louise. And I may call you Ellen, yes? For we are to be friends, are we not?"

Ellen smiled at her helplessly. "Of course."

Dobberham murmured to Edmund, "She's got every day planned down to the last detail. She gives us barely two hours in the morning to go hunting and fishing."

Lady Dobberham turned and gave him a smile. "You will enjoy it immensely, I promise! Everyone has accepted our invitations and the rest of the guests will arrive in the afternoon. In the meantime, Mrs Mills will show you to your rooms and you can refresh yourselves. It will be so exciting to have newlyweds at our party! Newlyweds in love! I have so many exciting pastimes planned."

"Lord help us," muttered Edmund as he followed Mrs Mills up the marble stairs to their room, while Noni was taken to the nursery.

THEY HAD A PROBLEM.

The room faced south, and the windows overlooked

the park. It was an exquisite room, hung with silky blue wallpaper and taupe curtains. Plush carpets covered the floor, and a massive gilded mirror hung over the fireplace.

Ellen had never seen a more beautiful room. It was perfect.

Almost.

The problem was the huge rosewood four-poster bed with its light-blue-and-gold silk damask drapery and matching bedspread, which was clearly the masterpiece of the room. To the left and right were oval bedside tables, each with a candelabra placed on a lace doily. At the foot of the bed was a pretty little sofa bench upholstered in taupe velvet. It was a dream of a bed, fit for a king.

She looked around and found, to her relief, a door to the right. A dressing room. Simple, plain, functional, with a wardrobe, a washstand and two chairs. Frowning, she returned to the bedroom. There. A tapestry door. Ellen stepped up to it, relieved. Surely this must be the second room with another bed. She pushed it open.

But it was another dressing room, slightly larger than the first. There were gilded mirrors on the walls, a wardrobe, a chest of drawers, and a screen with chairs. A tin tub stood by the window.

"That's it?" She turned to Tewkbury, who was watching her with hooded eyes. "Where will you sleep?"

He gestured to the bed. "It appears—here."

"But-but-but that won't work!" Ellen hissed.

"Hush."

A footman had entered the room, carrying her valise. It seemed that the dressing room on the right was hers, and the one on the left was his.

Both were staring at the bed. After the footmen had

gone, he pressed down with one hand to test the mattress. "I say. Don't see what the problem is? Seems big enough for both of us? Married couples are supposed to share a bed, you know."

He gave her a look so full of devilry that it left her speechless.

"You forget, we just have to pretend to be married in public. No need to keep it up in private."

"Indeed. Didn't count on Dobberham. He no doubt thought he was doing us a favour." Tewkbury frowned. For it was customary, even for married couples, to have separate bedrooms. "If we insist on separate bedrooms, there will be talk," he reasoned. "Remember, we are supposed to be madly in love with each other."

It was a complication she hadn't thought of.

"Does that mean we have to, er, you know? Share it?" She rubbed her forehead.

Just then, his valet entered, carrying his trunks.

Tewkbury looked at her warmly. "Yes, my darling, it does indeed."

The valet disappeared into the dressing room.

He lowered his head to murmur in her ear, "May I remind you I am paying you half a fortune for this? So do your best to play the part. What do you say, my love?" He raised his voice again, making sure it carried into the dressing room.

"I-I suppose I must agree." She looked at him doubtfully. "My l-love."

The corner of his mouth twitched. "If it makes you feel better, it's yours from midnight to six in the morning. Then till noon it's mine," he said in a lowered voice. "No need to worry. We won't even meet."

Ellen pondered on this bed-sharing plan. Could that work? She would have to get up even earlier, to get dressed. And she would have to make sure she went to bed on time, so she didn't oversleep. And he could have the bed to himself all morning if he wanted. It could work. Maybe.

"Unless you can think of something else? It is the only sensible solution," he said.

Ellen agreed. "Very well. Let us do so, in the absence of a better idea." She'd wondered what he would do all night, but that was hardly her problem.

"My lord, may I suggest the hunter's green for this afternoon?" The valet, Lionel, stood before them and lifted his coat.

Tewkbury raised his quizzing glass and waved it away. "No. 'Twon't do. Why are you always insisting on the hunter's green, by Jove?"

"Because we're in the country, sir?"

"When in the country, one can't dress in country colours," Tewkbury lectured.

"One can't?" Lionel looked bewildered.

"No, my silly boy. One will merge with the vegetation and be mistaken for a shrub. That can hardly be the purpose of high fashion."

Lionel swallowed. "Very well, sir. Let's find another coat, then."

Ellen had followed the conversation with confusion and watched as they disappeared into the dressing room.

That was her cue to change as well.

It was a good thing she actually had clothes to wear, and in retrospect she was grudgingly grateful that Tewkbury had insisted on buying her an entire wardrobe from Madame Minion.

Her maid, Annie, helped her into a lovely pale-green afternoon dress and brushed Ellen's ginger hair into a bun. It wasn't as severe as her usual hairstyle, and several copper tendrils floated around her face, framing it.

"May I say, your ladyship looks lovely in this dress."

"Thank you, Annie." Ellen smiled at her from the mirror.

Through the dressing room door, she heard the men's voices discussing waistcoats. The door was half open, and she glimpsed Tewkbury standing in his shirt and stockings as Lionel danced around him.

Ellen looked away quickly. It would take some getting used to; this invasion of each other's personal space.

"I suppose Tewkbury will be awhile," Ellen said. "I shall visit Noni in the meantime."

She fled.

Noni had been put in the nursery in another wing. His nurse, Susie, was with him, for she'd accompanied them to Dunworthy Manor. Noni stood by the window, two fingers in his mouth, watching the Dobberham children playing with wooden blocks on the floor. Ellen observed how he cautiously approached them, crouched down on the floor and picked up a block, playing quietly by himself.

Susie caught her eye. "He'll soon get used to his new surroundings. It will be good for him to be around other children."

Ellen agreed. Having seen Noni playing happily, she left to return to her room.

Tewkbury left the dressing room just as she entered. He stopped and posed.

Ellen was speechless.

He was a vision in pink. Salmon pink coat, rose waistcoat and flamingo-pink trousers. Even the handkerchief he'd pulled out to dab his nose with was pink. He wore a pink carnation in his buttonhole. And his cravat was mauve.

"Ah, my dear, there you are," he drawled, lifting his quizzing glass to study her new dress. "I say. Madame Minion's gown suits you to perfection. Something is missing, however. I wonder what that could be? Ah. I see. Lionel? Lady Tewkbury needs some carnations, too."

The valet scurried back to the drawing room and returned with two carnations.

"I'm not sure," Ellen began, "the pink will clash with my hair."

"Faradiddle. There is no such thing as clashing colours. Besides, my dear, remember that fashion statements are made by breaking conventions, not by bowing to them."

Her maid took the flowers and secured them in her hair with a few hairpins.

"Lovely." He regarded her approvingly. "Shall we, then?" He lifted his arm. After a moment's hesitation, she took it.

As he led her out of the door, she noticed that he'd lifted his arm and turned sideways, as if to sniff at her wrist. A puzzled frown formed between his eyebrows.

She wanted to ask him why he kept doing that. She'd washed her hands earlier, with the Pears soap provided.

But just then Louise came tripping towards them.

"Good, good, good, here you are! Tewkbury, don't you

look an eyeful? A veritable tulip. Or should I say rose?" She giggled. "You eclipse us all. The ladies would fall all over themselves, only, what a shame, you are married now! How tragic. No offence, Ellen. I can't wait to see what everyone says! Everyone else has arrived and is gathered below. We'll have such an entertaining afternoon, you will see!" she trilled.

"It will be a pleasure indeed," Tewkbury drawled. "I say, what can be more enjoyable than playing games, like little children? Harpy diem and all that."

Louise burst into laughter. "You are so funny, Tewkbury. *Carpe* diem it is, of course! Let this be the motto of our party. Come along!"

Ellen glanced at him to see if he was being sarcastic, but his face was a mask.

Strange, she thought, how he played the fool in the company of others.

She wondered why, and if she could find out if there was more to it while they were here.

CHAPTER TEN

*A*part from Tewkbury and Lord and Lady Dobberham, Ellen knew absolutely no one in the entire party. Louise introduced her to everyone, and she was interrogated and studied behind quizzing glasses with raised eyebrows. There was the Duchess of Amersbury, Lady Gosford, Lady Elinor, who nodded at her kindly, Miss Anne, who she was chaperoning, Miss Mary, Lady Cynthia, who snubbed her outright, and other ladies whose names she immediately forgot. Now she was sitting on a sofa next to the Duchess of Amersbury, who was talking to Lady Gosford, listening to them discussing the latest gossip at Almack's. She did not know any of the people mentioned, so she felt a little out of her depth.

Remember who you really are, Ellen reminded herself. You are a schoolmistress. And proud of it. She lifted her chin. If she could handle a room full of unruly school-children, she could handle a room full of frightful aristocrats.

She had nothing to be ashamed of, even if the Duchess

had spent a terrifying moment inspecting her through a lorgnette, remarking that her hair was quite red.

Well, it was. One couldn't help the colour of one's hair, even if one washed it daily with St John's wort and mullein. It was a recipe her nurse had insisted she use on her hair since she was a little girl, and somehow she'd kept doing it until now. It was supposed to make her hair more flaxen, but so far it had made little difference.

Lady Gosford looked down her narrow nose at her. "One hears that you and Tewkbury had a rather hasty marriage."

"Yes, I suppose it was rather precipitous." Ellen plaited her dress under her fingers. "Some things can't be helped, I suppose." It was an awkward answer, but what else was she to say? And where was Tewkbury to help her out of this predicament? He was in another corner, chatting with two other ladies who had their hands over their mouths and were giggling. He seemed very popular with the ladies.

Lady Gosford's eyes fell on Ellen's stomach. "One can imagine what that might be."

Ellen stared at Lady Gosford, stunned. "Oh. No. It's not that at all," she stammered. She clasped her hand to her stomach, which might not have been a wise move.

Louise's face broke into a delighted grin. She leaned over to Lady Monroe, who was standing beside her, and whispered in her ear. Lady Monroe's head turned towards Ellen. She winked.

Ellen stifled a groan. Wonderful. Now it would spread like wildfire that they'd married because she was pregnant.

Fortunately, the footman rolled in a side table with tea

and a selection of sandwiches, seed cakes, hot crumpets, Madeira cakes, ham pies and sausage rolls.

Eating was good because it meant less talking.

"Yes, eat, eat, child. It is good for you and the little one," Louise said. "Amazing how one's appetite grows, don't you think? Every time I am increasing, I eat like a whale." The Dobberhams had three little ones, all under the age of three.

"It's not what you think," Ellen protested.

But Louise merely patted her arm.

During tea they'd asked about her background, and Ellen had found it difficult to answer without fibbing while giving enough information to satisfy their curiosity. The closer to the truth, the better, she decided.

When the Duchess of Amersbury had asked who her parents were, no doubt expecting some titled lord, Ellen had replied, "Mr Jacob Robinson. My stepfather is a professor of philosophy and literature."

"A professor." Lady Amersbury had paused for a tiny second before bringing her teacup to her lips. There was a world of censorship in her words.

Ellen chose to ignore it.

"I'm sure Lady Tewkbury means her sire is a learned gentleman scholar of the landed gentry," put in another lady whose name Ellen had forgotten.

"Oh, no." Ellen took a sip from her teacup and set it down with a cheerful smile. "My stepfather taught at Cambridge for the last decade or so, but now he lectures at the Royal Institution and writes books."

"He makes his own living?" Lady Gosford gasped.

Ellen sat up, her spine straighter than a pole. "Why,

yes. It is nothing indecent. I am used to making my own living too."

The room was so quiet you could hear the clock ticking.

"You... are used to making your own living," the Duchess said haltingly. "Pray. How?"

"I am a schoolmistress. That is, I was until recently, that is, before I, er, married Tewkbury."

"A schoolmistress!" A look of horror crossed the Duchess's face.

Miss Anne clapped her hands over her mouth. A sneer crossed Lady Cynthia's face. She leaned over to Miss Mary and whispered loudly for all to hear, "It seems Tewkbury has married grossly beneath his station. A *mésalliance*."

The Duchess seemed at a loss for words. "But, my dear..."

Only Lady Elinor, an elderly widow who was Miss Anne's guardian, found nothing wrong with what Ellen had said. "Schoolmistress." She nodded curtly. "Where, pray?"

"In Bath."

Lady Elinor nodded. "Of course. You must be one of Miss Hilversham's teachers."

Ellen gave her a quick, curious look. "You know Miss Hilversham?"

Lady Elinor tutted. "Of course I do. Runs the finest seminary in the country. With the choicest teachers. They say they are all ladies of impeccable breeding. The girls there are not only ready for the marriage market; they are well educated."

Ellen felt her eyes well up with relief and gratitude. She'd received support from a most unexpected quarter.

It was amazing what a difference Lady Elinor's pronunciation made. There was a palpable change in the atmosphere.

"Miss Hilversham! But hasn't she married the Duke of Rochford? I read about it in the papers." Louise looked at Ellen with renewed interest. "He was such a wicked scoundrel before he married. Do you mean to say that you know the Duke and Duchess of Rochford personally?"

That would be a very different matter indeed, wouldn't it? To be in the same social circles as a duchess. It would elevate her tremendously.

"Of course. Miss Hilversham, Her Grace, the Duchess of Rochford, is my employer," Ellen finally admitted. "That is, she *was* my employer. Before I married Tewkbury." She kept forgetting that she was supposed to be married.

Only Lady Cynthia wasn't impressed and wrinkled her nose. "It's generally said that it's not wise to turn a lady into a bluestocking and fill her head with useless learning when her aim in life is to marry. I know of no gentleman who would like such a lady, let alone marry her. Such a woman has no chance on the marriage market."

"So they say," Ellen replied sharply. "It is a common malady in our society to believe that the less educated a woman is, the better her mind will be. The opposite is the case. And our school is proof that education need not stand in the way of a good marriage, for this is another common misconception. People tend to think that well-educated women are incapable of attracting a husband. Well, Miss Hilversham's seminary has thoroughly disproved that fact. Our bluestockings marry very well indeed."

"The Duchess of Ashmore was a pupil at the same school, am I right?" Lady Elinor came in to support her again. "As was the Duchess of Morley and the Duchess of Dunross. They say," Lady Elinor turned to her eager listeners, "that any girl who goes to that school will inevitably end up marrying a duke. Any sensible person would have said that was nonsense, but the facts speak for themselves."

"Well, some of them have married viscounts or lesser nobles," Ellen felt compelled to say, but on the whole what Lady Elinor said was true. Her school had produced an inordinate number of duchesses, and they said that it was due to a wishing well on the school premises. It was all rubbish, of course, but it had become part of their school legend.

"But I feel it is important to point out that this is not the main purpose of our seminary. We are not marriage brokers or matchmakers. Our aim is not to marry off our students to the highest bidder. If our students end up marrying well, it is because of the excellent education they receive. It is almost equal to the education given to men, which is unparalleled in any school in the kingdom."

"You speak with conviction." Lady Elinor nodded. "If I were young again, I would have wanted to attend such a school myself, instead of being married off at the tender age of sixteen, having the first child at seventeen, the second at nineteen, and so on and so forth." Lady Elinor had nine children in all. "And what you have done, young woman, to teach in such a place and bring up such bright, young women, is indeed to be commended. It takes a considerable amount of fortitude and intelligence to do so."

"Thank you." Ellen looked gratefully at the older woman.

"Oh!" Miss Anne looked at her with wide, blue eyes. "My parents tried and tried to get my admission to the seminary, but we were turned down every time. Miss Hilversham, that is, Her Grace, said they had no capacity for any more pupils. I was heartbroken, for I had my heart set on going there, and if at the end of the school I were to end up matched with a duke, that would have been fine indeed, though my main motive would have been to enjoy the education there, which I, too, heard is superior. My parents sent me to another finishing school, which is quite inferior to Miss Hilversham's Seminary in Bath. How delighted I am now to meet one of its teachers!" Miss Anne sat next to Ellen and looked at her with something like admiration in her eyes.

Ellen shifted uncomfortably. "Well, yes, I'm afraid Miss Hilversham has had to turn down many applications because the school has reached capacity. She only has so many teachers…" And now Miss Hilversham had lost her too. A pang of guilt shot through Ellen.

Within minutes, Ellen's status in the group had changed drastically. Her bourgeois background forgotten, she seemed to be seen in the light of a 'duchess-maker'; someone who held the secret ingredient to attracting a duke, so that if one rubbed sleeves with her, some of that magic might rub off on them.

Miss Anne sat to her right, Miss Mary to her left, and she found herself surrounded by all the other young ladies who wanted to know more about the seminary. What they really wanted to know, of course, was how to catch a duke. Ellen sat back and decided to enjoy this sudden improvement in her status. Anything to make her life easier, she told herself. After all, the afternoon would be here soon enough, and then they would be playing entirely different games.

CHAPTER ELEVEN

*A*fter tea, Louise announced everyone should go outside. "For the weather is most pleasant, and I have planned some entertainment!" The children were already frolicking on the lawn.

Ellen raised her hand to shade her eyes and saw that Noni was trying to do somersaults with the other children. She smiled.

Lady Dobberham had planned a game of croquet, bowls and boccia. That wasn't too bad, Ellen decided. She knew how to play croquet; she played regularly with her pupils, and she wasn't half bad at it. Bowling was more of a man's game, although she would like to try throwing a bowling ball, and boccia was something she was familiar with too. As long as they were playing, she wouldn't have to talk. Or so she hoped.

The first hour went well, and Lady Gosford won, followed by Ellen. She'd swung the mallet and hit the ball cleanly through the hoop.

"What an excellent swing," said Monteroy, a tall lord

whose face wore a perpetual sneer. "Where did you learn to play croquet like that?"

"At the seminary," she was about to say, but she bit her lower lip just in time. She did not want to perpetually remind them that she was, or had been, a schoolmistress. "I liked to play with my brothers and sisters," she replied instead.

There were more refreshments under a tent. Next to it was a circle of chairs.

Louise clapped her hands. "Ladies and gentlemen, we will now proceed with our next game…"

Ellen was ready to crack her knuckles and try her hand at boccia.

"…Seated Buffy!" Louise beamed at her. "With modified rules. The object, ladies and gentlemen, will be for you to find a particular person—blindfolded. The ladies shall sit, while the gentlemen will have to guess the identity of the person by sitting on her lap."

The ladies shrieked. The gentlemen groaned.

"And pray, who shall decide which person we have to find?" drawled Monteroy.

"I shall." Louise lifted a silk handkerchief. There was an impish look on her face as she walked around. "As Mistress of Revels, I'll also choose my first victim. The first person to play is…" she paused for a moment in front of Mr Ellington, a handsome gentleman with tawny hair and a shy smile, who raised both hands in horror. Louise laughed and walked on, stopping in front of the man next to him. "Tewkbury."

He pulled a face. "Spare me, Louise."

"Oh no! You are the perfect one to start the game. Your task is to find…" Her eyes swept down the row of ladies.

Ellen felt an uncontrollable urge to hide.

Louise's eyes fell on her. "Lady Tewkbury," she said triumphantly.

"That should be easy enough," Tewkbury said, turning to allow Louise to tie the blindfold over his eyes.

He stood in the centre of a circle of chairs in which all the ladies were invited to sit, but once his eyes were blindfolded, everyone scampered off to change places.

"Ready?" Louise spun Tewkbury around until he protested. "Faith, I don't know up from down," he complained as he groped his way forward. His knees bumped into Miss Anne's legs, and she giggled.

"Begging your pardon ma'am, but I shall have to sit on your lap." He sat gingerly on her lap.

She clasped her hands over her mouth to squelch a laugh.

Edmund smiled. "Ellen doesn't giggle like that. Next." He groped his way to the next chair, where Lady Gosford sat. This time he did not sit, but he touched her shoulder; his fingers trailed down her arm, and he lifted her wrist to his nose. Lady Gosford made a funny sound in her throat. Edmund dropped her hand.

"That must be Lady Gosford, I think," he murmured.

"Amazing!" she exclaimed. "How did you know?"

"Lily of the Valley by Floris."

"That's right! What an excellent nose you have!"

He bowed and stumbled on to the next person.

The lady in the next chair raised her hand to his nose before he could move.

A slow smile spread across his lips. "Jasmine and vanilla. The base note is white cedar, to balance the sweetness. The scent is called Elegance, a special combination from Adonis. I congratulate you on your exquisite choice of perfume, Miss Elinor. It is the best on the market at present."

Her hands fluttered to her bosom. "It is, isn't it? I was lucky to obtain a bottle, for they were well sold out by the time I left the shop. The brand is quite new."

"What did you say the perfume was called?" demanded the Duchess.

"Elegance by Adonis. It is notoriously difficult to get a hold of. For some reason, the company only produces a certain number of bottles."

"I must have a bottle," exclaimed the lady sitting next to Miss Elinor. "How could I miss it?"

"Hush, Miss Mary, you have given yourself away," Edmund scolded, walking past her. She pouted.

He stepped to the next lady, who did not offer her hand.

She tilted her head up and fluttered her eyelashes. She looked up through her lashes and drew her mouth into a tight smile that was somehow... intimate.

Ellen knitted her brows together.

"Lady Cynthia, of course," Edmund murmured, not even bothering to take her hand. "Nothing sweet and floral for you. Citrus and bergamot."

The lady smiled, satisfied, and looked up to meet Ellen's eyes. There was a gleam of triumph in them.

How strange.

Lady Lorena and Lady Watson he identified without a problem, for one wore a scent of violets, the other lavender.

Then he stood before her.

Ellen held her breath.

He put one hand behind his back, extended the other and leaned forward as if asking her to dance. Her heart pounding, Ellen put her hand in his.

"A soft, gentle hand," he murmured. "Tender as a bird's."

He lifted it to his nose, but as he did so, he turned her wrist. His thumb rubbed over the delicate skin. Something irresistible rushed through her veins.

"Ah, of course. My Ellen."

His voice was a deep caress. Her heart made a funny lurch, then refused to return to a normal, regular pattern.

"Amazing, Tewkbury, amazing. Of course, one would know one's beloved by her scent. And now, tell me, what perfume does your wife wear?" Dobberham demanded.

Tewkbury's nostrils flared, and Ellen felt his warm breath on her skin. Small goose bumps formed on her arms, and she held her breath.

"None." He frowned. "It's not perfume, it's soap. Pear soap, like you keep in our rooms. It smells like an English garden."

"Correct," Ellen whispered.

Louise nodded. "Plain water and soap are often best for the complexion, I find. And Gowland's lotion."

"I swear by Olympia Dew," Miss Anne put in.

The general conversation drifted towards cosmetics. Edmund removed his blindfold, but there was a line between his eyebrows.

"And there is something else I cannot identify," he murmured.

Ellen tilted her head to the side and looked at him quizzically. But before she could ask him what he meant, Lady Dobberham had chosen her next victim. It was now the gentlemen's turn, and Miss Anne had to wear the blindfold.

They played several rounds and Ellen was tired. These games might be amusing to children or those looking for potential mates, but she'd had enough. There were loud shrieks, giggles, and laughter, and things escalated when Lord Benton, a dashing dandy, could not find the lady he was assigned to find and had to relinquish a forfeit.

A few minutes later, everyone rose to go to the refreshments table, where Ellen gratefully drank a glass of cool lemonade.

"We'll take an hour's break, then we'll get ready for dinner," Lady Dobberham announced, clapping her hands.

The ladies returned to the drawing room with their sewing frames, while the men stayed outside to drink.

Ellen stood in the corner of the drawing room and realised that she didn't have a sewing frame. She did not teach sewing at the seminary; that was another teacher's speciality. Ellen hated sewing and tried to avoid it whenever possible. But now, as all the ladies sat on the sofas, their heads bent over their sewing frames, she wondered what she should do in the meantime.

Reading was one possibility.

She stepped outside to find the library.

"One moment, please, Lady Tewkbury." Lady Cynthia had followed her. She was a tall, stately woman who carried herself erect. Perfect ringlets of golden curls covered her head, not a single one out of place, with a pale pink ribbon threaded through them. Her neck was swan-like, and her white muslin dress made her look both girlish and Diana-like. She was one of the men's favourites.

And she had flirted with Edmund.

Her lips were now curved in a smile that held a hint of malice.

Ellen drew her tongue over her lips and waited.

"I'm so pleased to make your acquaintance," she said, as if this was their first introduction, and they hadn't spent the whole afternoon together playing silly children's games.

"Likewise." Ellen folded her hands in front of her and looked at her steadily. The woman wanted something, and her instinct told her it was nothing good.

"I've known Tewkbury for a long time, you see." She traced the marble pattern of the column they stood beside with a delicate finger. "And he has never, as far as I can tell, had the interest or ambition to settle down in the marriage way. Which is why, you must understand, we were quite surprised to learn that he was arriving here—with wife and child. Knot tied, deed done. Rather sudden, don't you think?"

"Noni is his ward."

"Yes, so you say." Cynthia raised a delicately plucked eyebrow. "Interesting, isn't it? Edmund has never been interested in children, or women, or settling down. Until now. I find that strange."

"Love tends to change people," Ellen suggested gently, suppressing a wince as she uttered the lie.

"Love!" She let out a hard, cold, laugh.

Ellen's eyes widened in surprise. Was the woman jealous? If not, what on earth was wrong with her?

"Well, yes, love." Ellen held her gaze. "Why else would we have married so quickly?"

Lady Cynthia's eyes swept over her dress and stopped

at her stomach. Ellen had to force herself not to put her hand on her belly. Not again! Was that all these women ever thought about? Then it occurred to her that Lady Dobberham had already started the rumour.

A knowing smile crossed Lady Cynthia's beautiful face.

Well. Let her believe what she wanted. She did not have to defend herself in the least.

Ellen frowned. She was used to dealing with people. True, most of them were children or ladies growing into adulthood; but she'd also had her share of difficult parents who'd tried their best to intimidate her, but inevitably failed.

"Edmund is not the type of man to commit himself to one woman. There has always been a good, shall we say, *understanding* between us, and I'll do my best to keep it that way."

A subtle threat ran through her words.

Ellen pulled herself together. She was a schoolmistress. She would not be bullied by anyone. Especially not by this Lady Cynthia.

"And what, may I ask, is that to you, Lady Cynthia? You are, if I may say so, almost impertinently personal, insinuating things which is generally considered to be rather bad mannered."

That sat. Ellen watched with satisfaction as a red blush crept across Lady Cynthia's cheeks. Ah, so she had not lost the ability to make adults feel like helpless school-children. More power to her.

"I'm sorry if Tewkbury raised some expectations that he was unable to fulfil," Ellen continued. "I am truly sorry if you have been disappointed in that regard. But it is what it is, for life is like that sometimes, and things do not always turn out the way we expect."

"I'll not be lectured by you," Lady Cynthia hissed. Her eyes narrowed to slits and for a moment, her face became a hideous mask.

Ellen had to stop herself from flinching. Then a streak of fury raced through her. How dare that woman speak to her like that?

"I am his wife, Lady Cynthia," she said in a voice she usually reserved for her most rebellious pupils. "It would be best if you accepted that. Now, for the sake of peace, while we both live under the same roof, I suggest we both forget this unpleasant conversation ever took place."

Lady Cynthia's face slipped back into its usual serene mask. "Of course, if you insist, we can pretend otherwise," she murmured.

Ellen ignored her words and hurried away, her heart pounding, and her palms sore from digging her finger-nails into them.

Who did this Lady Cynthia think she was? Was she a former lover? A woman spurned? Did Edmund really have some sort of arrangement with her that he'd failed to fulfil...? But then why had he not turned to her for the purpose of this ridiculous charade?

Question after question.

CHAPTER TWELVE

*T*he evening would not end. After 'Blindman's Buff,' Louise led them through various parlour games, such as 'musical chairs' or 'Poor Kitty.' They were innocent, if not childish, games, and most of the guests played along good-naturedly.

Edmund, however, knew Louise and the ultimate purpose behind her entertainment. He knew as the night wore on, and the alcohol flowed more freely, these games would become less innocent, especially when it came to the payment of forfeits for those who'd lost.

Edmund had had the good sense to double up on everything: two pocket-watches, two quizzing glasses, two flowers, and two handkerchiefs. Woe to those men who only had one pocket watch with them. They would soon run out of forfeits. For eventually, they would have to take off their shoes and cravats, followed by their boots, their coats... even their waistcoats. Edmund had seen men stripped down to their undergarments and made to kiss not just one, but all the ladies in the room.

Edmund breathed a sigh of relief that he'd had the good sense to show up with a wife.

As for the games, Edmund had been lucky so far. He'd been declared the winner of 'Blindman's Buff,' and during 'musical chairs' he'd managed to grab a chair every time the music stopped. He'd only lost one game so far: 'Poor Kitty,' because Ellen, of all people, had been his partner and he'd failed to make her laugh. She'd kept a straight face throughout the game, even yawning once, and no amount of meowing and flattery had brought a smile to her face. He'd even tried to rub his head against her arm, as cats were wont to do when they wanted attention, and he'd meowed pitifully. While everyone else had burst into uncontrollable laughter, Ellen had looked at him with a haughty, schoolmarmish expression. Louise had finally declared her the winner of the game.

He had to pay the forfeit, and dropped one of his pocket watches into the basket Louise had provided. It was already full to the brim with fobs, rings, pendants, two pairs of shoes, a cravat, and even a coat.

Ellen, so far, had not paid any forfeits. However, she hadn't smiled for the rest of the evening. She looked pale and tired, and there was a deep furrow between her eyebrows. Edmund wondered if she was ill.

Louise clapped her hands. "Time to cry forfeits!"

"Excellent," muttered Mr Tilney. "That means we can spend the rest of the evening playing cards."

Edmund gave him a satirical look. "This is your first time here, isn't it?"

Mr Tilney confirmed.

Edmund refrained from saying that the actual game

had only just begun. He poured himself a glass of Madeira and sat back in his chair, legs and arms crossed.

Louise tapped her finger on her lips. "Let's see. You know the rules? You must redeem your forfeits properly or not at all. I shall personally oversee this process and ensure that all penalties are paid. Mr Tilney, you are first."

Mr Tilney jumped up from his chair and rubbed his hands. "Very well. Let's get on with it! The sooner we can finish and move on to a game of cards, the better."

The gentlemen agreed.

"Stand here, Mr Tilney, and accept your penance: 'Bow to the wittiest, kneel to the prettiest, and kiss the one you love best.' And mind you, no kisses on the hand or cheek." Louise's eyes twinkled. "It must be a proper kiss on the lips."

The men laughed. The women blushed. Mr Tilney's face was priceless. "But..."

"No butting around, Tilney. Be a man! The best thing is to get it over with," said Monteroy.

"Very well." Tilney walked over to Louise and bowed. No one could contest that she was the wittiest in the room. Then he knelt down in front of Miss Mary, who was pretty indeed, a delicate flower with a pale complexion. Mary stepped back and blushed. And then, whispering an oath under his breath, he stepped up to the lady next to her, Miss Anne, begged her forgiveness and planted a quick kiss on her astonished lips.

Everyone roared. The men slapped him on the shoulders. Tilney, his cheeks flushed, dared not meet Miss Anne's eyes, which sparkled.

Louise smiled, satisfied. The first couple had been matched.

So it went, penance after penance, all involving kisses in the most creative ways. Some gentlemen who'd been given the penance of kissing the lady of their heart chose to kiss all the ladies in the room rather than reveal where his true heart lay.

"Is it always like this?" Mr Tilney wiped his brow. He'd just kissed Lady Eleanor, who insisted on a proper kiss, not just a mere peg.

"The worst is yet to come," Dunstan prophesied.

And so it was.

Lady Cynthia had to kiss Monteroy as many times as she guessed his age; if she got it wrong, she had to start again. Predictably, she got it wrong.

Miss Mary had to kiss the candlestick that Mr Ellington held in front of his face. He cheekily removed it, so that she ended up inadvertently kissing his lips.

"Tewkbury." Louise picked up his pocket watch.

Edmund rose with a sigh of resignation. "I humbly await my penance."

"Only one item to redeem. Tonight was your lucky night, indeed. I shall see that tomorrow is very different."

Edmund did not like the cunning look on Louise's face.

"And since Lady Tewkbury also has only one item to redeem," she lifted a pendant, "I'll come up with something particularly challenging. You and Lady Tewkbury will 'Kiss the Monkey'."

Edmund groaned.

"What's the matter, Tewkbury? You should have had enough practice, being in the middle of your honeymoon, " Lord Benton announced with a gleeful chuckle. He was a portly man with a flushed face from too much drink.

Ellen stood in front of Edmund, her cheeks flushed, avoiding his eyes. "Turn around and get on your knees," Louise ordered. They both knelt on the floor, back-to-back, and interlocked their arms.

"Now kiss."

This was easier said than done. Each had to turn their heads the other way, twist their upper bodies back and somehow get their lips to meet.

Her sweet, floral scent filled his nostrils. A lock of her hair fluttered across his lips. He turned his head, and she turned hers at the same time, and they crashed against each other.

Edmund winced. The crowd howled.

"Try again," Louise ordered.

He took a big breath, and his lips brushed her temple, soft as silk. He felt her mouth against his chin.

"Doesn't count. Missed! Try again! Really, you two, one would think you'd have more practice by now," Monteroy scolded.

Edmund could feel Ellen's body quiver with embarrassment.

"It's not that simple," Edmund growled. The problem was that Ellen was a good head smaller than him. He would have to lower his head. She raised hers. A second attempt. This time he reached her cheek, and she reached his.

The third time was no better.

"No good! No good at all!" Louise exclaimed amid the general hilarity. "Try again."

He twisted his neck further until he felt a crack in his spine, lowered his head further — sweet heaven, that smell—and his lips groped for hers. Finally, their lips brushed together swiftly.

It was over before he realised it, and he let her go.

Louise crossed her arms with a discontented expression on her face. "That was a chaste kiss. The kind I give my brother when I kiss him goodbye. It won't do at all. Since it took you a good four tries to fulfil this very simple penance, I am afraid I shall have to add another penance to top it."

"I say, Louise, that's not fair," Edmund protested. "We've done our penance, so that should be enough."

"My dear Tewkbury. I am Mistress of Revels here, so I reign over this evening and determine its rules. And I decree that you two will show the rest of us how to kiss properly. You see," she raised her hands sadly, "we simply do not know how to do it. You are a couple deeply in love, so show us how it's done!"

"Aye, that's a good one," Lord Benton nodded, raising his quizzing glass.

Ellen stared at Edmund, eyes wide.

He scratched his neck.

Dash it all.

"Play along," he murmured, "the more you resist, the worse ideas she'll concoct." Turning to the crowd, he said with a mocking smile, "Very well, watch closely and learn."

Then he swept her into his arms and bent her backwards, one hand supporting her neck, the other cupping her waist. Her lips gave way beneath his, and he kissed her deeply, his mouth moving over hers in a lazy, sensual exploration. Her lips opened fully, and he pressed her closer to him. Deeper. Deeper. There was heat and pain and sweetness, an intoxicating sweetness... A small moan escaped her throat.

He tore his mouth away and buried his face in her hair to catch his breath.

There was silence in the room.

Lord Benton had dropped his quizzing glass.

Miss Anne stared at them with her mouth wide open.

Lady Gosford had one hand clasped over hers.

Lady Cynthia's eyes flashed with fury.

Ellen looked up at him, her mouth red and raw, as thoroughly kissed as a woman could be, her eyes wide and dewy.

"That, ladies and gentlemen, was a proper kiss." His voice sounded somewhat hoarse.

Monteroy clapped slowly.

The others followed.

Edmund ran his hand through his hair. Poor Ellen, redder than a strawberry, pulled on her shawl and did not know where to look.

Edmund threw her an intense look, then announced, "I'm sure you'll excuse us, now, for a newlywed couple has more important things to do than play parlour games all night."

And amidst a great deal of hooting and whistling, he lifted Ellen into his arms and carried her out.

CHAPTER THIRTEEN

"*Y*ou can put me down now." Ellen's voice was not quite steady.

He lowered her carefully, but held onto her hand as he quietly led her up the stairs and into their room.

As the door closed behind her, Ellen remembered with a jolt the arrangement of their room.

Just one bed.

Someone had pulled back the covers, plumped the pillows and made the bed ready for the night.

Edmund leaned his back against the door and sighed.

Ellen whirled round to face him. "Did you know it was going to be like this?"

"Of sorts," he admitted.

"Of sorts! I know these games are all too common in certain circles, but I didn't know it would be this bad."

Edmund looked at her wearily. "Why do you think I insisted on coming here married? Louise is hell-bent on coupling everyone who is here."

After a moment's silence, Ellen said, "Lady Cynthia seemed unpleasantly surprised that you were married. I wonder if she herself had certain expectations?"

Tewkbury looked up quickly. "Lady Cynthia? Expectations?"

"She seems to think you had some sort of understanding."

"Does she? She's commonly known to be a fortune hunter, and I count myself lucky that she didn't have a chance to sink her teeth into me. Besides, it hardly matters now that we're married. "

He was right. Something relaxed in Ellen.

"Will it be like this for the rest of the stay?"

"It will get worse."

"That's terrible! What do we do now?" She gestured at the bed. "I thought we agreed that I was to have the bed until morning."

Edmund pulled out his pocket watch. "From midnight until morning, yes, but it's barely ten. We'll miss supper."

Ellen's stomach growled.

"We could have a tray brought up, I s'pose." He strolled to the dressing room and disappeared.

Ellen rubbed her forehead. She could sit in that chair and read a book for two hours. She lit the two candelabras on the bedside table, placed them on the small table in front of the window, arranged her chair, fished her favourite book, a well-thumbed leather volume, *The Arabian Nights*, out of the trunk and opened it.

But somehow she found herself reading the same paragraph repeatedly.

She felt a wave of crimson heat wash over her body as she remembered the kiss. She placed her hands on her hot cheeks, remembering the sensation of his lips on hers. She'd never felt anything like it. Afterwards, there had been a glazed, languorous look in his eyes when he'd looked at her. Not proper at all.

This entire party was not at all proper, Ellen concluded. This high society, these fine lords and ladies of quality, who claimed to be the champions of civility and good breeding, behaved rather badly when they had the chance. Under normal circumstances, it was frowned upon for a man and a lady to be alone together in the same room. It could seriously damage a lady's reputation, and unless he married her, her prospects of marriage would be ruined.

But in society, especially at this house party, under the guise of a parlour game, the single ladies kissed all the gentlemen without as much as blushing, while their chaperones sat snoring in a corner, and it all seemed quite acceptable.

It was a paradox she did not understand.

Ellen chewed her bottom lip as she thought. It was a kind of matchmaking, Tewkbury had explained; perhaps he was right. She could picture Miss Anne and Mr Tilney together; and after Mr Ellington had kissed Miss Mary, a rosy blush had crept into both their cheeks. There were already two couples who seemed to match.

Clever of Louise, really.

Ellen put down her book and stood up. After a moment's hesitation, she stepped to the door of the dressing room and pushed it open.

Tewkbury stood at a table with a pile of clothes in front of him, humming to himself.

"What are you doing?"

He looked up, startled. "Sorting my cravats."

Indeed. The cravats were neatly folded and stacked.

"Though I must say it's an easier task in daylight." He lifted a pistachio green cloth with a frown. "It's quite difficult to tell in the dim candlelight whether this colour goes with this pile or that." He pointed to two piles of cravats in different shades of green. There was also a burgundy, creamy yellow, black and a white pile. Next to them were shirt fronts, ruffled, laced and ruffled, and an even larger stack of waistcoats.

"I'm trying to come up with more original combinations, you see," he explained as he paired a satin waistcoat, heavily embroidered with little flowers, with a burgundy cravat.

"Not bad," said Ellen. "The cravat goes well with the little flowers in the waistcoat."

"Exactly. That would be the conventional choice." He put the burgundy cravat to one side and chose a mustard-yellow tie. "But this? This combination has never been seen before."

Ellen shook her head. "Most gentlemen wear white cravats," she suggested.

"Precisely. Yet I am not 'most' gentlemen. I have had these cravats made especially for me."

Ellen concluded that she would never understand the mind of a fop.

"I thought it might be a good time to call for a tray of food," she suggested.

"What time is it?" he asked.

Ellen glanced at the clock on the mantelpiece. "Almost eleven."

He shook his head. "Too early."

"Really. What for?" She was hungry, and the longer she thought about it, the less she understood why they had to hide in her bedroom while the other guests were eating supper.

He lowered the cravat in his hands, and a slow grin spread across his face. "A night of passionate lovemaking that lasts only half an hour is rather pathetic, don't you think?"

Ellen stuttered.

SHE ENDED UP READING TO HIM TO PASS THE TIME.

He'd suggested it, and she'd agreed, opened her book and read the story of Sinbad. She'd read it countless times to her students at the seminary. This would be no different, she told herself.

But several times, her voice wavered as she read. She'd had to clear her throat and read the sentence again.

He sat in a chair across from her, his hands clasped behind his head, one booted leg crossed nonchalantly over the other, his gaze fixed on the ceiling.

Ellen paused to study his face.

He'd washed his face, and he looked so much younger without the patches of blush and heavy kohl under his eyes. He'd taken off his cravat and shrugged into a silken banyan, lavishly embroidered with red and blue flowers. His dark hair was tousled and the first few buttons of his shirt were undone.

He met her gaze with a question in his eyes. "And? What happens next?"

"He returns to Baghdad, and shortly after that he embarks on his second journey, which is even more fantastic."

Tewkbury was silent. "Lucky Sinbad. What a life to be able to travel the Seven Seas so carefree, lurching from one adventure to another."

"I don't know. Reading about it is one thing, but I wouldn't want to experience being attacked by monster whales, giant birds, snakes, or other horrible creatures. Sinbad always escapes and returns with riches, but I wouldn't want to go through that. That is what our imagination is for, and we can relive it all in books." She clutched the leather volume to her chest.

Edmund shrugged. "I have a good imagination without books."

"You don't seem to read much, do you? I noticed you don't have any library. It appears you have no books at all in your house."

That must have been the wrong thing to say, because the unguarded, carefree expression on his face disappeared as an invisible mask slipped over it.

"I have no time to read, ma'am. I am a busy man and have better things to do with my time." He got up. "I say. Enough time will have passed. I'll have a tray sent to your room."

He bowed stiffly and left the room.

Ellen stayed behind, wondering what it was about her words that had caused him to take offence.

Sometime later, a housemaid knocked on the door and brought a massive tray with white soup, fish with wine sauce, a savoury pie, and a slice of chocolate tart with fruits and marzipan. It was divine. Having eaten, she prepared for bed and crawled between the sheets.

She had six hours to sleep.

She wondered what he would do for six hours.

Play billiards and get drunk, probably.

CHAPTER FOURTEEN

*E*llen woke up an hour early, readied herself, and left the room. She met no one on her way downstairs and wondered where Tewkbury was. The entire house was quiet, and the early morning sun had not yet risen above the horizon. She went down to the dining room and found that breakfast was not yet ready as the footmen were setting up the sideboard. Ellen sighed. What a nuisance. She figured the rest of the guests would be asleep until midday, which meant she would have to amuse herself until then.

As the weather was fine outside, she decided to go for an early morning walk. She fetched her coat and set off.

The air was crisp and clean, and the birds were singing.

She walked around the lake, into the adjacent woods, and followed a forest path that led to a pretty little gazebo in the middle of a clearing. After a brief rest, she had no desire to return. Most of the house would still be asleep.

She could finish walking through the forest and then she'd be able to see what was on the other side.

When she came out of the forest, she saw a meadow with a stone fence, and she stepped over the fence. Her goal was the hill with a massive oak on top. There she would rest and then turn back.

The morning sun had grown quite strong, and Ellen took off her cloak as she walked. Beads of sweat trickled down her back.

When she reached the top, she bent over and put her hands on her legs, gasping for breath.

Once her breathing returned to normal, she took in the landscape below her. Another stretch of forest and another smaller lake, and in the middle of a garden with geometrically shaped bushes and fountains, stood a magnificent Elizabethan manor house of grey stone, with turrets and tall windows.

"Oh." Ellen sighed.

"It's quite a sight, isn't it?" a female voice said. "Penwick Hall."

Ellen whirled round.

There, in the oak's shade, a woman sat on a small wooden bench. Ellen hadn't seen her at first because she seemed to merge with the tree.

The woman was wearing a blue walking dress, but instead of a cloak, she had a shawl draped over her shoulders. Her fine brown hair was streaked with grey and there were fine lines around her eyes as she smiled at Ellen. "You must be one of Dobberham's guests."

"Yes. Yes, I am." Ellen remembered her manners. "I am Lady Tewkbury."

The woman's eyes widened, and her mouth opened slightly. "You don't say. Did I hear that right? Tewkbury?"

"Yes. We are newly married, Tewkbury and I. In fact. I don't think it's been announced in the papers yet." She supposed Tewkbury would have sent an announcement, or maybe he'd forgotten in all the excitement.

The lady was silent for a while, studying Ellen. "Congratulations," she said at last. "Forgive my surprise, for this is most unexpected. None of us could have imagined it — but very well. Come here in the shade and sit with me." She patted the spot next to her on the bench. "You must be quite hot from standing in the sun."

"Indeed, it doesn't do my freckles any good, either." Ellen said wryly.

The woman laughed a pleasant, low laugh.

Ellen sat down beside her.

"So you married Tewkbury. Good for him!"

"Do you know him well?"

The woman waved her hand. "Of course I do. Everyone does. He visits Dobberham often. And none of us ever expected him to get married, hence my surprise. You seem like a lovely woman."

"Thank you." Ellen pulled a face. "It takes some getting used to; being married, that is."

The woman nodded sympathetically. "I suppose it does. Any change in one's station in life takes some getting used to. But tell me, how is he? Is he well?"

Perhaps Ellen was imagining it, but there was a glimmer of sadness in the lady's blue eyes. But it was gone in an instant and the fine lines crinkled again as she smiled.

"He's doing well enough, I suppose."

The lady nodded. There was a pause. "Dobberham, or rather his wife, must be keeping you busy. Their parties are notorious."

"Yes." Ellen jumped to her feet. "And I had better get back before I'm missed."

The lady held out her hand for Ellen to shake. "I have enjoyed making your acquaintance, Lady Tewkbury. I was wondering if you might return here in the next few days, or at least some other time before you return to London, so that we could continue our conversation?"

"I suppose so, as it is a most delightful walk, and I, too, have enjoyed it very much."

"I was wondering," there was a note of hesitation in her voice, "if you are in the habit of walking with your husband, and if you might come this way again. Because it would be a pleasure to see you again. And your husband too, of course," she hastened to add.

"I don't see why not," Ellen said cheerfully. "It would give us an excellent excuse to escape some of Lady Dobberham's dreadful parlour games."

The woman smiled again, and it struck Ellen what an amiable lady she was.

Ellen walked back to the mansion on light feet, happy to have made a new friend. It was only much later it occurred to her that the woman had not introduced herself.

CHAPTER FIFTEEN

*T*ewkbury strolled into the room dressed from head to toe in red and pink, causing a round of titters from the ladies. It was nearly noontime, and the guests were gathered in the dining room, where breakfast had been laid out on a sideboard. Ellen looked lovely in a green morning dress. She looked up from her plate with kedgeree and smiled shyly when she saw him.

"Good morning, my love," Tewkbury murmured, planting a kiss on her forehead. "I've missed you."

She blushed.

"By Jove, you two love turtles cannot bear to be apart for more than an hour, can you?" joked Dobberham. "For my part, I am more than content not to see my second half for most of the day, although I miss her most at dinnertime." He shot an affectionate glance at Louise.

Some of the men had been out hunting and had returned red-cheeked and in good spirits. Tewkbury hadn't joined them. He'd had something better to do, for he'd spent a good part of the morning in the nursery.

At first, he'd told himself he'd only take a short peek to see how the little fellow was doing. He'd found Noni quietly playing with wooden blocks on the floor, somewhat apart from the other Dobberham children, who were jumping and screaming around him. Something about the way the boy had bent his curly black head over his toys had tugged at Edmund. He knew exactly how it felt to be the odd duck in the room. Then, just as he was about to retreat, Noni had seen him. He'd run over and thrown his little arms about his waist. Edmund had a strange lump in his throat as he tousled the boy's hair. Then Noni had pulled him into the room, back to his wooden blocks, and before he knew it, he'd crouched on the floor next to the child, building a tower that was higher than the table.

Strange how quickly time passed with such an activity; and he found it infinitely more entertaining than any of Louisa's games. Noni had looked at him with big, questioning eyes.

"I say. No need to look so sad," Edmund had told him. "I'll be back, I s'ppose."

It had squeezed his heart to see the boy's eyes light up at that pronouncement.

Somewhat disturbed, Edmund had returned to his room, just in time to change. He'd have to check on the little fellow more regularly from now on, Edmund told himself as he pulled on a fresh waistcoat; but somehow he preferred no one knew about his new pastime, including Ellen.

When Ellen had looked up to see Edmund entering the room, her heart had skipped. She thought he looked well rested, whereas Ellen felt she needed a nap after a morning with the ladies. There was no time for that, however, for Louise asked them to gather in the green drawing room after breakfast. The afternoon lay before them with a series of never-ending games.

"We shall play 'tableaux vivants' today," Louise announced. "I'll put you in pairs and you have to pull your theme out of a hat." She lifted her husband's top hat, which she'd turned upside down. Inside were slips of paper with topics. "Your task is to put together a tableaux vivant using the items you have been given. Miss Anne, you and Mr Tilney are a couple."

Both blushed and looked away.

"Lady Tewkbury, I'll pair you with..." her gaze swept over the group, pausing for an infinitesimal second on Tewkbury, then moved on to rest on the gentleman next to him. "Ainsley. Yes. Two redheads in a tableau should make a striking vision."

Mr Tilney nudged Lord Ainsley, who appeared to be dozing with his legs crossed in the corner of a Chesterfield sofa. He'd had too much to drink the night before, missed the morning hunt, and turned up for the afternoon's entertainment half asleep, his shock of fiery red hair dishevelled. He was dressed in sober clothes and seemed a pleasant enough fellow. It was clear to all that he was smitten with the lovely Miss Mary, but had been too ashamed to kiss her to redeem his forfeit when he'd had the chance. Instead, he'd planted a shy kiss on her wrist, causing the rest of the gentlemen to roast him for being a coward. Only Tewkbury had not teased him.

"What's happening?" Ainsley looked around, blinking.

"You are to partner with Lady Tewkbury and create a lovely tableaux vivant."

"Oh. Splendid." He threw Tewkbury a doubtful look. "Husband doesn't mind?"

Tewkbury scowled at him. "I do indeed. I say, Louise, I insist on being paired with my wife. I can't bear to have a fool like Ainsley as her partner."

"Nonsense. You two lovebirds spend far too much time together, which I must say is very understandable under the circumstances," she clasped her hands and fluttered her eyelashes at him, "for you are newlyweds and very much in love. It is so charming, doubly so, as love matches are not at all common in our circle. But it is time for you to suffer some time apart. Some distance will increase the longing between you. I have therefore decided that you, Tewkbury, will pair with Lady Cynthia."

Lady Cynthia looked smug, ambled up to Tewkbury and took his arm. "I am pleased. We are certainly well-matched." She blinked her eyelashes at him. Edmund merely laughed.

Ellen felt a quick stab in her heart.

With a mischievous grin playing around her lips, Louise held out a hat. "Take one," she said to Tewkbury.

He pulled out a piece of paper and passed it on to Lady Cynthia, who smiled.

A roar of laughter and protest had everyone looking in the direction of Miss Anne and her partner, who had just pulled their slip of paper.

"Really, Louise?" Mr Tilney's face was one of mock despair. "How on earth are we to replicate this?"

Louise handed him a copy of an etching. "Like this, and no other. Choose your costumes well."

Then she held out her hat to Ellen, who drew a piece of paper. "The love letter."

Ellen showed it to Ainsley, who scratched his head. "I don't think I'm familiar with this piece of art," he confessed.

"Neither am I."

"I'll give you a clue," Louise whispered into her ear. "The library."

The two looked at each other, then rushed off to the library. Once there, they surveyed an oil painting from the previous century that hung above the fireplace.

"It can't be this one. Isn't there another painting?" Ainsley turned to look around the room, but apart from a portrait of Lord Dobberham's father, there was no other painting.

"Louise must have made a mistake," Ainsley began. "Because I see two women in that painting."

"Yes, indeed. There are two women. But I don't think Lady Dobberham was wrong." Ellen stifled a sigh.

The two women in the painting were seated, one with an arm around the other. They were dressed in tightly laced, low-cut gowns from the previous century, and one held a letter in her hand, the other a quill.

The corners of Ellen's mouth twitched. "Well, which of the two lovely ladies would you like to impersonate? The one without shoes and stockings, holding the letter; or the one with the low decolletage with the quill in her hand?"

Ainsley sighed. "I'll be the one with the quill, gazing into the distance with lovelorn moon eyes."

He took on a dramatic pose, looking tragically at the ceiling, which made Ellen laugh.

The clothes they were to use were in a trunk by the desk. Ellen held up a purple dress and a corset.

"You'll have to ask your valet to help you lace the corset, for I certainly won't," Ellen told him.

"Heaven help me. I don't think my valet even knows how to tie a corset." Ainsley groaned, picked up his pile of clothes, and left.

Ellen wondered how Tewkbury and Lady Cynthia were faring as she made her way back to her room to change.

The tableaux vivants were performed before dinner, and Ellen had to admit it was entertaining. Most of the performers put a great deal of effort into recreating a still scene, which was a direct imitation of a painting or other work of art. The audience had to guess which one it was. Since Ellen had taught art history at the seminary, she found it relatively easy to guess most of the scenes; however, she stopped herself from blurting out the answer each time.

The subjects were true to Louise's mischievous nature, bordering on the improper. Miss Anne and Mr Tilney did an excellent job of portraying Persephone and Hades. Both were dressed in Greek costume; Mr Tilney in a black armour that looked as if it had been taken from Dobberham's mediaeval collection, and Miss Anne in an improvised Greek dress that looked lovely on her. Mr Tilney lifted her on his shoulder, and she leaned back and draped her arm over her forehead. They remained in this position for several minutes in perfect silence, without moving, but Miss Anne must have weighed more than Mr Tilney could carry, for his knees buckled under him and they both fell to the ground.

A roar of laughter and applause followed.

This was followed by a re-enactment of a more daring French engraving of a couple dressed in beautiful rococo clothes. Miss Mary and Mr Ellington depicted a kissing couple. Lady Esther, who'd been asked to take part as an extra, was dressed in a shepherdess's costume and looked on serenely.

No one in the audience knew the name or creator of the work of art they were trying to emulate, so the couple froze in the kissing position for quite some time.

"Probably something to do with a kiss," Bentley guessed.

"Almost, but not quite," Louise replied.

Ellen knew the answer, as they'd been studying French art last term. "First Kiss of Love by Noel Le Mire."

The couple broke apart, gasping for breath.

"I swear it was the longest kiss ever," Monteroy concluded.

Miss Mary's cheeks were red, but she smiled, and Mr Ellington returned the smile.

Ellen and Ainsley were next.

"The humiliation," Ainsley grumbled as he pulled the bodice up, and Ellen had to fight to keep a straight face.

"You make a lovely lady, miss," she said, adjusting the ribbon in his hair. The dress was too small for him, and in the end he'd left off the corset because his valet couldn't get him into it.

Ellen was grateful that their tableau vivant wasn't as

risque as Miss Anne's and Mr Tilney's, for she wouldn't have liked to have been half-dressed and lifted by a man.

All they had to do was lean against each other, with Ainsley's arm draped around hers, stay in that position, and that was it. No kissing, hugging, or any of that nonsense.

When the curtain rose, they were greeted with gasps, laughter, and whistles.

"Oh, look at that. Doesn't Ainsley make a pretty dish of a girl," exclaimed Lady Elinor.

Ainsley fluttered his eyelashes and pretended to use the quill as a fan.

"You're supposed to be still," Ellen hissed.

Although she was wearing a pretty pink dress with a laced bodice over a corset so tight she could barely breathe, she wasn't wearing shoes or stockings and felt strangely underdressed. Her legs were exposed down to her lower calf.

Tewkbury stared at her bare feet, which were crossed at the ankles and stretched out in front of her, and her whole body began to prickle. Ainsley pressed his arm tighter around her shoulders and she could feel his breath on her neck.

Tewkbury scowled.

He was playing the role of the jealous husband all too well, Ellen thought.

"Now, ladies and gentlemen," Louise announced, "what painting could this be?"

"I've seen it somewhere," Dobberham scratched his head. "The question is, where?"

"The two shepherdesses," Miss Anne guessed.

"One is holding a letter, the other a quill, so my guess is 'The Missive,'" Lady Cynthia suggested.

"Very clever, but not quite," Louise said.

"Oh, I know, I know!" Miss Mary clapped her hands and jumped up and down. "It's that picture in the library. I saw it the other day when I went to get a book to read."

Dobberham scratched his neck. "Drat. Is it? Considering I see it every day, I must be blind not to recognise it."

"The Love Letter, by Francois Boucher, of course," the Duchess of Amersbury guessed correctly, "for there must be some improper element in it."

"There's nothing improper about love letters, is there?" Miss Anne protested.

Happy that their performance was over, Ellen and Ainsley parted company.

Tewkbury walked up to him, shoved him on the shoulder, and hissed something in his ear.

"'Crikey, Tewkbury, it wasn't meant like that," Ainsley protested. But he was met with a thunderous glare.

What was that all about? Ellen wondered. But she didn't have time to ask, for next up were Tewkbury and his partner.

And what they represented caused the entire audience to gasp.

Lady Cynthia, dressed in a Greek gown, stiff and proud, leaned back and raised her arms in a dramatic gesture.

But Tewkbury was—naked.

He had only a single white sheet draped over the crucial parts of his lower body as he lay languidly on his side, leaning on his elbows.

Ellen felt her jaw drop.

His torso was finely chiselled, the shoulders broad, the muscles rippled, revealing a powerful but lean body with a well-sculpted chest.

"My goodness, look at him! He is a Greek statue come to life!" exclaimed Lady Gosford.

"It's a pity he's already taken, ladies, isn't it?" cackled Lady Elinor.

"Not fair, not fair at all," complained Benton, "now all the ladies here will fall in love with him, and he's off the market."

Louise clasped her hands in front of her and looked at them rapturously. "Splendid." She sighed. Then she turned to the audience. "Now, what are they trying to portray?"

"Dido and Aeneas," one guessed.

"Amor and Psyche," suggested another.

Wrong on all counts.

The scene looked familiar, Ellen thought. But what could it be?

Miss Anne jumped to her feet with a shriek. "I know! How silly of me! Of course it is! I drew it myself only a fortnight ago. It's a scene from the Elgin Marbles, isn't it?"

Louise nodded, pleased. "Well done, Miss Anne, very well done indeed."

"Tricky one," Dobberham murmured, "as most of the sculptures have no heads nor arms."

Louise clapped. "Yes, but they did such a wonderful job. I congratulate you. And how difficult it is to choose a winner. You have all done a phenomenal job, and my works of art were difficult to recreate. But if I had to choose one that stood out above the rest, it would be..." she paused dramatically, "Tewkbury and Lady Cynthia's

Elgin Marbles, followed by Miss Anne's and Mr Tilney's Hades and Persephone, although you did not hold that position for more than a minute. And finally, The Love Letter by Lady Tewkbury and Lord Ainsley. Ainsley was a delightful sight as a woman."

Ainsley, who still wore women's clothes and seemed to have taken a liking to them, fluttered a fan he'd borrowed from Miss Anne and curtsied. "I am delighted, Lady Dobberham," he said in a falsetto voice.

CHAPTER SIXTEEN

$\mathcal{B}$y the end of the first week, Edmund was deeply sorry that he had agreed to come to the house party. He should have just packed his bags and gone on a trip. He could have gone to Bath to take the waters, or to the Lake District, or even to Scotland. At worst, he could have fled to France.

Oddly enough, he enjoyed the daily stolen moments with Noni in the nursery, which reminded him of the time when he was young and ran about the house and park together with Dobberham. They'd scampered through forests and fields, swam in the lake, and fished in the brook.

It was because of Dobberham that he was here, he reminded himself. He was his friend; the only friend he had who knew what Edmund was really like.

The other gentlemen regarded him as a ninnyhammer, and that was fine with him; he was used to being seen by society as a fool who wasn't quite right in the head. He

SOFI LAPORTE

suspected he'd contributed to that image. Only with Dobberham did he let down his guard.

Despite appearances to the contrary, Dobberham, like Edmund, was not given to excesses in gambling, drinking or womanising. And though he liked to boast to the contrary, Edmund knew his friend was faithful to Louise and worshipped the ground on which she walked.

The others, however, spent most of the night gambling and carousing, casting up their drinks under the table, only to imbibe more.

It was distasteful, to say the least.

Edmund made sure he never drank more than a few glasses, especially since his last drunken escapade appeared to have resulted in him being saddled with a ward. Now, some of the men shouted rowdy songs and suggested that they should all go down to the wine cellar, where there would be even more wine.

If he could, Edmund would have retired to his room long ago.

Only there was a woman in his bed, and that woman was his wife.

They had said vows in a church without meaning them. It had felt real, and yet it had been a lie. The whole situation made his head spin. He wouldn't say he regretted marrying her. There were some parts of the arrangement that were convenient. He no longer had to watch out for the unmarried misses or endure the fear that he might end up shackled to one of them. That had been the whole point of it all, hadn't it?

And then there were moments in his marriage when it felt all too real.

Like now, when he stood in front of their bedroom,

stepping from one leg to the other, knowing his wife would be inside, sleeping.

Hang it all. He wanted a bed; he wanted a quiet, dark room, and if Ellen was there, so be it. She was supposed to be his wife, after all.

He opened the door carefully and stepped into the room.

She was asleep. The covers tangled around her, her red hair spread across the pillow, and a hand was tucked under her chin.

She looked like a little girl when she slept.

Edmund stood in front of the bed, stunned, barely able to tear himself away from the vision. With a sigh, he peeled off his coat and cravat and stretched out in the armchair by the window. He cast off his shoes and propped his legs up on the second chair. It was uncomfortable, to say the least, but he was so, so tired. He tucked a small, hard, decorative pillow under his head and dozed off.

Sometime during the night, he found himself lying on the floor.

It was hard; he was cold, and he was shivering.

Someone tugged at his arm and pulled him up.

Someone pushed him onto the bed.

He sighed with relief as he was surrounded by warmth, and the arms around his neck were soft. There was more of that soft sweetness that sparked heat; that made his whole body thrum and burn. He took a deep breath and buried his face in a divine mass of silky hair. Then his mouth sought hers, yielding, demanding.

He burned with sweet longing, agony, and bliss.

He was lost.

As the first rays of the morning sun crept between the curtains, Edmund felt Ellen untangle herself from his embrace and slip quietly out of bed. She tiptoed to the dressing room, as if not to awaken him. But he'd already been half-awake for the better part of the hour, pondering on the preposterous notion that maybe a real marriage wasn't as bad as he'd thought it would be. He could get used to sharing his bed with her, even though she had the tendency to mumble in her sleep and pull the entire blanket to her side.

Edmund grinned.

While she dressed, he got up, pulled on his banyan and drew aside the curtains. The sun flooded the room and a feeling of contentment, almost of peace, washed over him. It was a feeling that was all too rare, when one knew that all's right with the world.

She came out of the dressing room and stopped short when she saw him. How lovely she looked in her green walking gown. "Good morning," she stammered, and fiddled with the ribbons on her bonnet.

"Are you going out?" he enquired.

"I was thinking of going for a walk. It is quite nice outside this time of day." She hesitated. "Would you like to join me?"

An early morning walk, where he'd end up getting his hair ruffled by the wind and his boots dirtied by mud and other muck that commonly lay about in the countryside?

"Why not?" he replied, surprising himself.

She gave him a bright smile. "I found a most beautiful path that delighted me the other day. Come, let me show you."

And before he knew it, he found himself outside, his wife on his arm, taking an early morning walk.

She was so eager that it almost made him smile. She explained the park and the countryside to him as if he'd never been here before.

"And there, in the woods, is a clearing with the most charming little pavilion. There's a path that leads out of it to a little hill..."

He walked along good-naturedly, enjoying the sound of her voice, the pressure of her hand on his arm, the heaving of her chest as she walked up her hill.

"Look," she said, "isn't the view absolutely splendid? And down there is the prettiest manor house, like something out of a fairy tale with those dainty little geometric bushes and trees, though I dare say they only look so dainty from up here."

Edmund felt the heat in his body turn to ice as he stared at the mansion below.

And then he saw her.

Standing beside the tree, her hands clasped in front of her, she looked exactly as he'd remembered the last time he'd seen her: slender, of medium height, wearing a blue-grey promenade dress. Only her hair was streaked with more grey than he remembered, and there were fine lines around her eyes that had not been there before.

He grabbed Ellen's arm.

Ellen saw the woman at the same time as he did. "Oh! Good morning!" she said cheerfully. "As you can see, we made it after all. It was the most pleasant of walks."

But the woman ignored her. Her eyes were fixed on Edmund with a questioning, anxious look.

For a long moment, neither moved.

He pressed his lips together in a grim, tight line.

She held out a hand as if in supplication. "Edmund."

Edmund's grip on Ellen's arm tightened. He felt her flinch and look at him with a questioning gaze, but his eyes were fixed on the lady in blue.

The woman dropped her hand. "Edmund," she repeated quietly. "You look—look—" she was clearly searching for words to describe the citrus-yellow-salmon-blue splendour in which he was dressed that morning.

Edmund took the words from her mouth. "You look very well yourself, Mother." It came out glibly, politely and cold. No sign of the stammer, no sign of the old insecurity.

Ellen gasped. "Did you say mother?" She looked from one to the other.

His mother stepped forward.

She lifted her hands and pulled his face down towards her, studying it.

Her big brown eyes had become determined. "You are my son, after all," she murmured, planting a kiss on his forehead.

She hadn't done that in fifteen years.

The kiss burned on his forehead, and he became engulfed by her scent. Lavender filled his nose, and he closed his eyes for a moment. A familiar, homely smell, soft, powdery, the scent of the sunlight streaming over the meadow. The scent of his childhood. The scent of home. Something scratched at the back of his throat. He looked away and blinked.

Edmund raised a hand to his forehead and rubbed it.

"Mother. I..." he had no words. What did you say to your mother when you hadn't seen her for fifteen years? They were strangers now. Harsh words had been spoken the last time they'd been in the same room together. Words that had haunted him; that had robbed him of sleep. Until he decided to brush them off and become a new person with a new life.

He was an adult now, no longer a little stuttering boy. But being in the presence of his mother seemed to return him to that very state.

His mother let go of his face and took Ellen's hands in hers. "You must forgive my deception, but I was too over-whelmed to think when I met you yesterday. I am Lady Honoria Tewkbury." Her eyes twinkled as she said the words. "The Dowager Lady Tewkbury, I suppose, is what I must call myself now. For you have married my son, and the news has taken me rather by surprise. I saw the announcement in the paper this morning. I did not know you had married so recently, Edmund. My most heartfelt congratulations to you both."

Ah. So West must have finally sent in the announcement.

"Ah, yes, well. I say. So I got married," Edmund said redundantly. "This is Ellen, my wife. Ellen, my mother."

After Ellen had struggled to find her voice, she said, "I had no idea. How completely unexpected. But how happy I am to make your acquaintance, ma'am."

"Please. Call me Honoria. And I may call you Ellen, yes?" She still held her hands, but her eyes sought Edmund's.

Edmund looked down at his boots, shifting from one leg to the other.

"Are you coming home now?" she asked. "You don't have to stay. You could just come for tea. For half an hour..." her voice trailed off.

Edmund continued to stare at his boots.

"Edmund?" That was Ellen. Both women were looking at him, and for the life of him, he could not look up and meet either of their eyes. Because what he wanted to do now was run, and run fast.

"Surely we could come for tea this afternoon?" Ellen nudged.

"It's been so long." His mother clasped her hands together in front of her.

She was inviting him to tea in his own house as if he were a stranger, as if the whole mansion and the land beneath it didn't belong to him. "And Edward is there too... with his lovely wife. He got married too, on the same day as you. Can you believe it?"

An icy barb stabbed his chest. "Then the answer is no." He finally looked up. "It was a pleasure to meet you, Mother, and I'm glad to see you well. But I'll not meet Edward. Or his wife." He gave her a curt nod and strode down the hill.

Away. Just away.

He walked so quickly, he almost ran.

Ellen rushed after him. "Edmund!" She grabbed his arm as she gasped for breath. "Slow down. I can't keep up with you."

He stumbled over a root and slowed his pace.

"Who is Edward?" Ellen asked.

He walked on in silence.

"Edmund?" She tugged at his arm.

She would not give up, would she? He felt anger flare at her, perhaps unwarranted.

"My brother. My twin brother."

She stopped short as she stared at him.

He shook himself and walked on. "And that is all you need to know."

CHAPTER SEVENTEEN

*H*e had a twin brother.

Ellen's head whirled.

And he'd never told her.

He had a mother she'd met by chance and who had only now found out they were married. Otherwise, he wouldn't have told her.

Why?

And why had he not told her that Penwick Hall was his? It was his family home, for as Baron of Tewkbury, he'd inherited the house and the estate. From all appearances, it was lovely and thriving.

She seemed to recall, somewhat darkly, that he and Dobberham had been childhood friends and had grown up together. But he hadn't told her it had been on this land, or at least next to Dobberham's.

He'd brushed it off, saying that was all she needed to know. But that was nonsense, of course.

She had to talk to him about it.

He was her husband, and as far as Ellen was

concerned, the pretence had ended long before he'd stumbled into the bedroom the night before.

A slight smile played across her lips as she remembered how young he'd looked, how carefree, without all that paint, his hair in disarray. He'd been sound asleep, lying on his stomach across the bed, hugging a pillow.

There had been no pretence between them, just raw honesty.

She would insist on keeping it that way.

Yet, the entire day, following their walk, he avoided her. Finally, when he was on his way to the billiard room with the other gentlemen, she grabbed his arm and pulled him into the library.

"We need to talk."

"I say, we don't," he began.

"Hush." She placed a finger across his mouth. "You know we do, and you're just avoiding it because it's uncomfortable. But believe me, it won't get any better, so the sooner we talk about this, the better. Not just this business with your mother and brother, but also this." She spread her hands.

"This?" He tilted his head to one side.

"You. Me. Us. What now?"

The clock on the mantelpiece ticked loudly in the silence. The sun flooded through the library windows and for a moment, time seemed to stand still, until Edmund finally opened his mouth to echo, "What now?"

Ellen sighed. "We embarked on this marriage as a pretence. It is no longer. So what now?"

Edmund scratched his neck. "We have a week left here. We have to get through it, pretence or not."

"And your mother?"

"Well, you've seen her, she's fine." He stared sullenly at the pattern on the carpet.

"Don't you think that even as your wife—even if it is entirely, as you say, a pretence," she hastened to add, "that I should at least know a little about your family?"

Edmund shrugged. He looked away and shuffled his boots on the ground.

Just when she thought he'd never speak, he opened his mouth. "Edward and I don't look alike. He's taller and more handsome, and he's been gifted with brighter brains. But I am half an hour older and therefore the heir. That hasn't always been acceptable to my brother. Or to my father, who never made a secret of the fact that Edward was preferable. He was the better heir. The better son. He never embarrassed him. He's not a fool like me and, as far as I know, has never made a single mistake in his entire life."

"Oh Edmund." Ellen regarded him with compassion.

Edmund looked up and away, as if not seeing her. "There was an argument. Not a minor disagreement, but a big one. We were about to kill each other if Mother hadn't pulled us apart. I'd had enough and left. If Edward wants it all, he shall have it. What do I care? I never asked for it and I don't need any of it. But that's not the way the world works. Then my father died. I made my own way through life. Haven't seen the others since. The end."

There was silence.

Ellen grimaced. "I'm so sorry, that's terrible." She took his hand.

"Yes, well, now you know. And as lovely as Penwick Park is, I'd rather not set foot on it. Not even to do my mother a favour for a cup of tea, not while Edward is there. He seems to do an excellent job of looking after the place, so I'm not needed and they're better off without me." He shrugged again.

Sorrow filled Ellen's heart. So that was what was driving him: forevermore being measured against his twin and being found wanting. To escape it, he'd fled into the caricature he'd created of himself, exaggerating the characteristics of an empty-headed fool. All to hide from a world that had badly hurt him.

She lifted her hands to pull his face down and kissed him.

A small sound escaped his throat as he responded.

He was so familiar to her now; his scent, the feel of his arms around her, the strength of his body against hers.

"Oy, they're kissing again." A booming voice broke into her foggy mind.

They moved apart, but then Edmund pulled her back and held her by the waist.

Dobberham, Monteroy and Tilney stood at the door, grinning.

"If you could stop what you are doing for a moment and listen, please." Dobberman announced. "Louise has instructed us to find you, for the games are to continue. Are you ready?"

Edmund groaned. "Must we?"

"Yes, you must. The weather has suddenly changed, and it is raining, so we cannot go on the trip to the Gothic Abbey, and Louise has come up with an alternative programme. She says it will be a witty afternoon." Dobberham grimaced.

"We could play a game or two to please Louise and retire early," Edmund suggested, a gleam in his eye.

The men smirked and slapped him on the shoulder.

Ellen did not know where to look.

LADY DOBBERHAM'S CHOICE OF GAMES TODAY SEEMED MORE to Ellen's taste, for they were word games.

Ellen sat in her chair next to Edmund. She smoothed her skirt with a sense of relief. She was good at these games and hopefully, with some luck, she would not have to pay any forfeits.

They had to sit in a circle and answer random questions without using certain vowels.

That's easy enough, Ellen thought, as it was a game she used to play with her pupils at the seminary.

Thus, to everyone's amusement, when Tilney asked Miss Anne if she enjoyed kissing, she blushed and stammered, "Yes," only to immediately clamp her hand over her mouth because she'd used a word containing the forbidden vowel E. Her forfeit was the feather she wore in her hair, which Tilney removed with nimble fingers.

Ellen noted that Edmund seemed rather poor at this game. He was clearly not in the mood. Every time it was his turn, he gave the wrong answer, to the general amusement of the group.

For example, when Lady Cynthia asked him if he thought it was important for a man to be well dressed, a question that required him to answer by avoiding the letter A, he replied, "Of course, a man should always be dressed according to the latest fashion," and everyone shrieked.

"Tewkbury! Have you got any idea how many A's you have used?" Dobberham laughed.

Tewkbury folded his arms and shrugged. "I say. Three?"

Ellen noticed a blush had crept up his neck.

Another round of laughter.

Ellen drew her eyebrows together.

"This is delicious." Louise was standing in front of him with crossed arms. "Tewkbury, pay a forfeit equal to the number of A's in your sentence. Stand up and deliver."

Ellen thought quickly. She pulled a handkerchief from her sleeve and dropped it on the floor in front of Tewkbury. As he knelt down to pick it up for her, she bent down at the same time and muttered, "Seven." She took the handkerchief he held out to her.

If he'd heard her, he did not acknowledge it, but in the end, he handed over seven objects he was carrying. He threw two quizzing glasses, two handkerchiefs, one flower, and one snuff box into the basket and, as the hilarity reached its climax, he took off a silver cufflink and threw it in as well.

"Well done, Tewkbury. For a moment I thought you'd forgotten how to count as well as your ABCs," boomed Monteroy.

Ellen decided that she heartily disliked the man.

Lady Dobberham, Mistress of Revels, decided that they should move on to another game where they had to write words on slips of paper according to clues she gave them, and the result was read aloud.

It was during this game that Ellen's suspicions were

confirmed. She took the piece of paper Edmund had given her, on which he'd scribbled his response to Lady Dobberham's question regarding his favourite colour; and with only a second's hesitation, she corrected the spelling, which was 'pruple' — with the e upside down. Then she added a word of her own.

Her mind whirled.

Tewkbury sat with his eyes closed and an expression of boredom on his face, as if none of this mattered.

When Lady Dobberham announced they would now move on to the game "I love my love with an E", in which they had to complete sentences with words beginning with a certain letter, he stood up and stretched. "I've had my fill. Thank you, Louise. I don't feel quite up to it and will retire."

"But you can't just quit the game like that, good chap, you have to redeem your forfeits," protested Bentley.

"Keep them." Tewkbury turned.

"You're a dashed bad sport, Tewkbury," Monteroy complained. "Why should he get away with it when the rest of us can't?"

"You must at least redeem your forfeits," Louise insisted.

"I say. Must I?" he drawled.

"How about I redeem them for him and release him from the game?" Ellen stood up beside him. "Because no one should be forced to redeem forfeits if they feel unwell."

"That's not the way the rules work," Monteroy complained.

"What do you suggest, Lady Tewkbury?" Louise asked.

Ellen looked into the basket and sighed. It couldn't be

helped. "Let's keep it simple. I shall offer a kiss for each of the items and then he may be released."

The others clapped and agreed.

Ellen stepped up to Tewkbury. "Seven kisses," she whispered.

His eyes were deep and dark and brown, and she told herself that if she just kept looking into them, the others would retreat. She cupped his face in her hands and kissed him full on the lips.

"One," the others chanted.

Two, three.. some were soft and lighter than butterfly wings brushing rose petals, others were more awkward smacks, and as the number increased, the kisses grew longer and slower, and his eyes became drugged and glazed as he kissed back.

"…five…six…seven."

The last was the longest, sweetest kiss of all.

He almost toppled over.

Ellen steadied him, and they returned to their chairs. While the others clapped and laughed, Monteroy said they should change the penalty for forfeits because "it was getting rather boring watching them kiss", and another agreed, "What is so special about watching a married couple kiss?"

Thus, they retired to their room.

Edmund tugged on his cravat as he headed for his dressing room.

"Aren't you going to tell me about it?" Ellen went after him.

"Tell you about what?" His tone was cool and distant. "Isn't that enough, woman? I've already told you my entire life story. My family background of trouble and strife.

Must you dig deeper and deeper until you've uncovered every shadow in my soul? It's not pretty." He tossed the cravat off in one motion and threw it on the table.

She winced. "I meant about your difficulties with the written word."

He turned to her, a look of open hostility on his face. "So the schoolmistress has noticed, has she?"

She hesitated for a moment before answering. "Of course I would notice. There's no need to be defensive. I have taught quite a few students who have struggled with something similar. "

"I'm not struggling," he said flatly.

"I have noticed that you exchange letters and that the E is written in reverse."

"And what are you going to do about it? Hit my fingers with a ruler? Spank me across my bottom for every spelling mistake? Stick my head in a chamber pot and force me to write 'I am a dunce-head' a hundred times, and for each time I get it wrong, give me an extra ten lashes across the bottom, not just from the teacher but from each of your mates?" His eyes burned.

"Goodness, no!" Ellen's eyes widened. "Edmund! Is that what they did to you?"

He pulled both hands through his carefully coiffed mane in one, two, three powerful movements. He made no response and stalked to the window, where he looked out.

"How long have you had these problems?" She continued to probe. "How old were you?"

No answer.

She took a deep breath. "Can you... can you read at all?"

He whirled around with an oath. "Would you stop pestering me with questions that are none of your business? I am not one of your unfortunate pupils."

"I was just wondering..."

"No!" he roared, causing her to recoil in fright. "I cannot read! At least nothing that's longer than three words. I can't write, and I certainly can't spell for the life of me, and it's not for lack of trying. There must be something wrong with my brain, as my father tried to tell me day after day, hour after hour, minute after minute, ever since I left my mother's womb an unfortunate half hour before my brother, to everyone's regret. I cannot even remember something as simple as the ABC. I was born an idiot, a simpleton and a fool, not worthy to bear the name of Tewkbury. There, does that satisfy your curiosity?"

He'd raised his voice at her as if it was all her fault.

Ellen had gone pale, but she held her ground, folding her shaking hands in front of her.

"I see," she replied. She would have said more, but he cut her off.

"No, you do not see. None of your kind does. All you are capable of is walloping hapless students who are unable to perform to a ridiculous standard, and when they cannot, you punish and mock them for life."

"This is an unfair statement and very untrue. I would never punish a child. A child with learning difficulties, and believe me there are many, just needs additional help and much patience. Look at Noni. He doesn't speak, but with time I am certain he will. I am very sorry that you weren't given kindness, time, and patience when you needed it most."

But she might as well have been talking to a piece of furniture.

"The governesses, headmistresses and tutors have been the bane of my life. They are a breed of people I despise with all my heart."

"How ironic that you should now find yourself married to one," Ellen replied sharply. "Even if it is only a fictional liaison. And we both must have imagined the other night."

"Indeed. It would have been better if it had not happened." His face was a mask.

Ellen's lips turned white.

"The only thing that makes this situation bearable is that it is a farce." Tewkbury tore off his waistcoat, pulling off a few buttons.

"You should have thought of that before you came up with this ridiculous proposal," Ellen pulled herself to her feet. "I cannot change who I am. I am proud to be a teacher." She turned on her heel and headed for the door.

He waved her away wearily. "Ring for my valet, will you?" he instructed her.

In response, she slammed the door, which she found very satisfying.

She ran out into the woods, sat down on a small bench in the pavilion and wept.

Really, what had she expected? That he would change his mind about this farce and realise that he'd fallen passionately in love with her? Ellen took out a handker-chief and blew into it. That would never happen. She'd agreed to this marriage on the understanding that it would remain a pretence.

But things had changed between them. She could

continue to ignore it, as he was doing. Play along, stick to their agreement. Or? She stared into the forest as a new thought occurred to her. Or... she could fight for it. See if she could make something of it. Something real.

Deep down, she felt that was what she wanted.

CHAPTER EIGHTEEN

*I*nstead of going on her early morning walk, Ellen had spent the last few hours poring over the bookshelves in the library, thinking about the incident with Edmund. It wasn't unusual to meet adults who couldn't read, but it was unusual for a member of the upper class to be completely illiterate, for they were generally able to acquire the best education the country could provide.

Ellen wasn't sure that the word 'illiterate' was even appropriate for Edmund; perhaps he merely had a weakness in reading and writing, as many of her pupils did. Occasionally, one of them would mix up letters. One girl she'd taught last term had complained that the letters danced off the page, changing position as she read. She had difficulty associating the letters with the sounds they made. Such pupils, in Ellen's experience, required a great deal of patience and a different approach to teaching. They did not thrive on a rigorous curriculum with twenty or more pupils in the same group, but did better when taken aside and taught individually.

At Miss Hilversham's Seminary for Young Ladies, it had been Ellen's responsibility to work with such pupils. It was hard, bone-breaking work, but also very rewarding. She had a gift for adding a playful element that made lessons enjoyable. More than once, she would form a close bond with the pupil who would slowly, haltingly, learn to read. It was Ellen's special quest, for she believed everyone was capable of reading. No exception.

And here was Edmund, the Pink of the *ton*, who could not.

Ellen strongly suspected that, after several failures, he'd simply adopted the attitude "I can't read, so I won't even try". That would explain why he had no library; not a single book in his townhouse.

But what puzzled her was his behaviour towards her. She'd discovered his closely guarded secret, and perhaps he now considered her a threat. Her hair had stood on end when he'd talked about the abuse he'd suffered at the hands of teachers. Poor little boy.

Then there was the issue with his family, the estrangement from his brother and his mother. She'd found his mother, the Dowager Lady Tewkbury sympathetic, and Ellen would have loved to get to know his family better. Edmund, however, had refused, and there was nothing she could do about it.

If only she could help! But he wouldn't let her. What could she do?

The previous day, Edmund had ignored her all evening. She'd gone to bed at the usual time, but he hadn't come. She'd got up an hour earlier than she should have, but she'd fallen asleep on the couch in the library. Her back ached from the uncomfortable position, and she shivered because the fire in the fireplace had gone out.

She pulled her shawl around her shoulders as she stepped out into the hall, where Louise and her husband were greeting a newly arrived guest, a slim, medium-sized gentleman with ash-blonde hair. He had a classic profile with an elegant nose and a well-set mouth.

"What a pleasure to have you here, Mr Mattick, and just in time, for the gentlemen have not yet left for their morning shooting. I promise the next few days will be full of entertainment, and the ladies here will be so pleased to have another eligible bachelor amongst them!" Louise gushed over him.

"I'm delighted to be here, Lady Dobberham. I wouldn't have missed your party for the world." He lifted her hand and kissed it elegantly.

Ellen grabbed the latch of the door and held on to it as if her life depended on it. She felt the blood drain from her face.

It couldn't be. What was he doing here?

A figure from another life. Another time.

Stunned, she let go of the latch, and it snapped with a loud noise.

The heads turned towards her.

Louise smiled and beckoned her to come forward. "Ah. And this is the first of our ladies here. Lady Ellen Tewkbury. May I present Mr Robert Mattick?"

The same blue eyes, the same round cheeks, and golden curls like an overgrown cupid.

He stared. "It can't be. Ellen!"

"Robert." Ellen drew her tongue across her dry lower lip.

Oh, this was bad. This was very, very bad.

Louise raised a delicate eyebrow at their use of each other's given names. "You seem to have already made each other's acquaintance?"

Robert broke into a smile, walked over to Ellen, and took her hands in his. "It really is you."

She pulled her hand away.

"Lady Tewkbury now, a newlywed." Louise watched them with sharp, curious eyes.

He dropped her hands. "You're married?"

Ellen fumbled for words. "Well..." Dear sweet heaven.

He must never find out this is a sham. She lifted her chin.

"Yes. I am married to Lord Edmund Tewkbury."

"Well, this will be a very entertaining few days, indeed. Smile," he hissed at her as he forced a bright smile upon his own face.

She felt the corners of her mouth lift in a reluctant smile and wished a hole in the ground would open up and swallow her whole.

For Robert himself had once, so long ago, given her his promise of marriage.

CHAPTER NINETEEN

*T*he new chap was making moon eyes at his wife, and Edmund did not like it one bit. He sawed into his steak with such force that the knife scraped the porcelain underneath and threatened to break it. His wife sat next to the new guest, and Edmund sat across from them—what was that fellow's name again? Every time he looked up, he saw the man tilting his head towards his wife and talking. And talking. While she listened. And nodded. And listened some more. There was this pinched, absent-minded smile playing about her lips that he'd never seen before. Somehow it gave him a pang in his chest, which made no sense at all. Edmund stabbed at the peas on his plate as if they were at fault.

He hadn't known that more guests were expected at this party. The fellow apparently was an old friend of Ellen's. Edmund suspected he must have been more than that, judging by the possessive way he now placed his hand over hers. Then, as he spoke, he touched her sleeve and leaned forward to look deeply into her eyes.

He'd called her Ellen, not Lady Tewkbury.

Edmund growled. What right had this fellow to call his wife by her given name?

"Is the steak not to your liking?" Lady Cynthia fluttered her eyelashes at him.

She was a beautiful but cold woman who'd been trying to flirt with him ever since they'd arrived at Dobberham Manor. At previous house parties, they might have had an unspoken understanding; they might even have flirted with the promise of more. But he had made no overt move towards her, nor had he ever made any promises. When it came down to it, Lady Cynthia was not to his taste. She was too tall, too angular and too sharp, especially with her tongue. Her eyes were sharp too, and she had already noticed that the new guest was making moon eyes at his wife.

Lady Cynthia smelled of lemon and bergamot; not an unpleasant smell, except that she'd poured so much of her toilet water on her hair that it was overpowering.

"Mr Mattick seems to be rather well acquainted with Lady Tewkbury," she mentioned between two sips of claret.

Edmund shrugged. What could he say to such an obvious statement? If he replied he did not care, it would sound callous and not in keeping with the image of a newlywed in love. If, on the other hand, he responded with jealousy, it rankled because… well.

His fork fell on his plate with a clatter.

Surely, it can't be true?

He wasn't really jealous?

Not of this ill-dressed oaf.

Edmund raised his quizzing glass.

This was no gentleman of fashion, he concluded. His coat was well-tailored but he wore it badly, and somehow the cut did not suit his physique. Nor was his cravat tied properly; it was slightly crooked. Edmund shuddered. He would shoot himself before showing up at a dinner party with a badly cut coat and a twisted cravat. His own cravat, of course, sat to perfection.

The man wore an unimaginative perfume, which he identified as a brand from Floris. One of their cheaper brands.

But this, what was his name again? Attic. Hattick. Mattick.

This Mattick, who exactly was he?

He turned to Lady Cynthia and abruptly posed the question. Her face lit up, for she was the gossip of the party and knew everything about everyone.

"He's from the well-to-do gentry, heir to a considerable fortune. Quite a catch, in fact."

She played with her fork as she assessed Mattick through her cat-like eyes. Then she turned back to Edmund with a smile. "But some of us have higher aspirations." She batted her eyelashes at him.

"Indeed," Edmund replied absently.

There, he did it again. That blackguard! Mattick had put his hand over Ellen's and was smiling deeply into her eyes.

Edmund cleared his throat loudly.

They both looked up. Ellen pulled her hand away and looked at her plate.

Mr Mattick smiled cheerfully and raised his wineglass.

Edmund bared his teeth at him.

Cur.

"THAT HUSBAND OF YOURS, HE SEEMS THE JEALOUS TYPE, I gather," Robert murmured into Ellen's ear.

"Is he? I suppose he is." Ellen stole a glance at her husband, who'd been staring daggers at her throughout the meal.

"If looks could kill, I would be pierced like a sieve," Robert commented.

Edmund had scowled at her, gripping his knife as if he'd like nothing better than to stab someone with it; preferably Robert Mattick.

Ellen concluded he was playing the role of jealous husband well and focused on eating her foie gras. If only Robert would let her eat.

If only he would go away.

A strange iciness had gripped her heart, and her brain had stopped working. He'd been talking ever since she'd been assigned his table partner, but she'd barely registered his words.

When Mr Tilney brought up the name of Jacob Robinson in the general conversation that revolved around literary writers and philosophers, Ellen knew the moment had come.

"Did you know that Jacob Robinson is Lady Tewk-bury's stepfather?" Louisa dropped into the conversation. "You must be so proud of him," she turned to Ellen, whose smile was pained.

Robert's eyebrows rose almost to his hairline when turned to her. "Mr Robinson. Your stepfather. Really?" He didn't move a muscle in his face.

Her cutlery slipped between her sweating fingers. "Yes. Really." Her heart pounded loudly. She put down the fork and knife and lifted her glass instead, only to find her hand trembling.

His eyes were on her, mocking. For a second, she thought about begging him not to say anything. The emotions inside her raged and pride won. She would never ask anything of Robert Mattick again. Ever. Not even about this.

"Interesting," he murmured, and turned to his table partner on the left. Thankfully, he'd dropped the subject. For now.

Ellen breathed an uneasy sigh of relief, wondering what on earth she was going to do when he brought it up again, as he undoubtedly would.

Once upon a time, she would have hung on every single word that fell from his lips.

She'd fallen in love with him the moment her father had brought him home from the club and introduced them. He'd seemed so romantic, with his blonde, tousled curls, his crooked cravat and sloppily slung coat. He'd taken her hand, kissed it, and looked deep into her eyes. Her heart had skipped a beat, and she'd fallen in love with a depth and passion that only a sixteen-year-old girl who knew nothing about love was capable of. She'd worshipped the air he breathed, the ground he walked on. She'd even broken off a branch from a cherry tree in her front garden and cherished it because it had brushed his coat sleeve as he passed.

And then, one sunny spring day, on the day she turned seventeen, he'd called on her while her father was out.

"We get along famously, don't we, Ellen? So what do you think? Shall we elope?" He'd said it as matter-of-factly as if he'd suggested they take tea in the drawing room.

Elope. She'd thought it was a good idea, because her father would never approve of their marriage.

"Wait, my child, wait," he'd said. "Mr Mattick is certainly a fine gentleman," he'd added, "but not in your league. He is not for you."

Words she hadn't heeded... For with her heart in her eyes, she'd trusted Robert more than her father and had eloped with him to Gretna Green.

She crumbled the bread she was holding between her fingers.

Her eyes met Edmund's across the table; deep, melting, dark brown, frowning. He did not like Robert. That was clear. Or was he just pretending?

She wished he wasn't. She was so tired of all this playacting.

Edmund was dressed in particularly garish colours today. He was breaking a taboo, for gentlemen were expected to wear white cravats at the dinner table. His was burgundy. He was the only splash of colour on the entire dinner table, for the gentlemen were all dressed in black and white, while most of the ladies wore white. The same cut, the same colour, the same style.

For a split second, she understood why he did it. Of course. Why had she not seen this before? His fashion was simply a statement. "I'll not be like you," it said. "I don't care what you think of me. I refuse to conform."

"What do you think, Tewkbury?" Dobberham asked. "Of your wife's famous father, I mean."

Ellen looked up, startled. She'd been gathering wool and had missed the general conversation about her father's literary merits. How could she have missed it?

"Yes, Tewkbury." Robert leaned back in his chair and

crossed his fingers behind his head with a grin. "What do you think of Lady Tewkbury's famous father, Mr Jacob Robinson? I hear he is a philosopher and literary giant." His eyes glittered maliciously.

Edmund shrugged. "I say. What's there to think? I don't read, so it doesn't matter what he writes about."

"You don't think. You don't read. What do you do?" Robert scoffed.

"Fashion and perfume." He wiped an invisible crumb from his sleeve. "How does the famous proverb go? 'Man is his waistcoat.'"

"He means to say, 'Man is his clothing.'" Dobberham winked at him as he raised his glass. "Or more commonly, 'Clothes maketh the man'. A saying which is undoubtedly true."

Robert pursed his lips in contempt. "Wise men speak because they have something to say; Fools because they have to say something."

Edmund's face brightened. "I know that one." He snapped his fingers. "It's by that Greek fellow whose name is that of a porcelain dish." He pointed at his plate. "Plate."

"Plato. Well done, Tewkbury." Dobberham grinned at his friend.

"Him? You really married him?" Robert whispered in Ellen's ear.

"Yes, him." She put down her fork and knife and turned to him.

"Why, Ellen? When you could have had your pick amongst the most intelligent men in the country?" The unspoken phrase was, of course, "When you could have had me."

Ellen sat up and glared. "You really have the nerve to say that?"

He opened his eyes wide. "But, my dear Ellen. It was all a terrible misunderstanding, nothing more."

If she could, she'd smash her fork into his hand and scream. Instead, she took a deep breath. "Because, Robert, he gives me something you never could."

He looked at her in confusion. "I wonder what that could be?"

She watched as Edmund fiddled with the creases of his cloak.

A warm feeling ran through her.

"Love."

CHAPTER TWENTY

*O*f course she'd lied.

It was a white lie, born of the circumstances of the moment.

But it worked. Robert withdrew with a strange look on his face, as if she had somehow betrayed him.

It was all nonsense, for she had never betrayed him. It was the other way round: he had betrayed her.

And in the worst possible way.

She had sworn she would never forgive him; and now, ten years later, she sat next to him at a house party, pretending that nothing had ever happened between them so long ago, and that she was now married to the man sitting across the table from her.

Ellen felt a headache coming on and wanted to go back to her room, but Edmund intercepted her and took her arm possessively. He frowned at her.

"If you tell me to smile, I'll scream," she warned.

"I'll say no such thing. But you do not seem very well. That Mattick must have said something to upset you."

Her eyes shot up to meet his. She hadn't expected him to be so perceptive.

She waved him away. "An old acquaintance... of my father's. It adds another complicated layer to this charade and makes it difficult to maintain our own pretence. Can we not cut this visit short and just leave? You have made your point. Everyone here is convinced that you are married. It seems to me that neither of us is happy here. So why stay?"

He ran a weary hand through his hair. "Because I promised Dobberham. But perhaps you are right, and it would be better for us to cut it short. We could leave tomorrow."

Ellen looked at him with relief. "Thank you."

"The child may object," Edmund said. "He seems to like it here."

Ellen gave him a surprised look.

"I visited him in the nursery earlier," he explained.

"You... visited him in the nursery?" Ellen blinked.

Edmund shrugged. "Thought I'd keep an eye on the little fellow. Doesn't know anyone here, doesn't speak. Thought he might feel a mite lonely. But I saw that he's made friends with Dobberham's children, though he still refuses to speak."

Ellen had also checked on the child daily and would never have imagined that Edmund had done the same. She felt a warmth spreading through her chest.

"That is very nice of you to think of the welfare of the child."

"He and I might have some things in common." Edmund tugged at his cravat. "I say. I'll inform

Dobberham of our decision. Then it's just a matter of getting through this evening's entertainment."

At first, everything seemed to go smoothly. Louise had decided on riddles and asked each participant to draw their partner from a slip of paper.

Tewkbury, however, stubbornly refused to draw a name and put his arm around Ellen's shoulder. "We'll be partners."

No amount of persuasion or cajoling could change his mind.

The riddles went well, because Ellen had memorised almost an entire book of them from using them with her students. Since she knew most of the answers, she won.

"It's not fair," Miss Mary complained, "because Lady Tewkbury clearly has the advantage over all of us."

Robert, interestingly, had not done well. He had laughed and thrown forfeit after forfeit into the basket, as if he didn't care that he had lost.

He was the first to redeem them, too.

"Kiss the one you love best," Louise told him, which was by now a predictable request, and Ellen would have thought nothing of it if it hadn't been Robert.

"Oh dear," Robert muttered, turning around in a circle of giggling women, "who shall I choose?"

Many men in this position would simply kiss more than one woman to keep their true love a secret, but not Robert. No.

Of course, he would choose her.

"Lady Tewkbury." He stood before her, his eyes glittering.

Ellen stiffened.

A ferocious growl emerged from Edmund's throat.

"It's just a game, isn't it?" Before Ellen could protest, Robert took her in his arms and planted a kiss on her lips. That should have been enough, but the problem was that he went deeper.

He wasn't nearly as good a kisser as Edmund. Not even close. Then it occurred to her he was kissing her longer than he should, and when she tried to pull away, his grip on her tightened.

Ellen struggled.

He increased his grip.

A roar. "Let go of my wife, you cur!" Suddenly she was released. A thud echoed through the room, and Robert sprawled on the floor, stunned.

Everyone jumped up.

"It's only a game, Tewkbury," Dobberham began.

"This game ends here," Edmund snarled. "He took advantage of the situation. I saw it."

"Nonsense." Robert touched his eye as he got up. "She enjoyed it."

"I most certainly did not!" Ellen gasped.

Edmund swung his fist and hit the other eye. Robert staggered backwards and nearly crashed into the fireplace.

"The devil!" Robert gasped. "This is too much." His eyes were blood-shot, and red marks appeared immediately.

"I demand satisfaction!" Edmund would have thrown himself at the man on the spot, but Dobberham came between them.

"Nonsense. Edmund, stop it now." Dobberham pulled him away. "What on earth has got into you? This is only a game, and I'm not having duels and bloodshed at my house party." He lowered his voice. "He's not worth it."

"No duels." Ellen grabbed Edmund's arm. "Let's just go home. Please. Now."

Edmund stared at her pale face, then gave a curt nod.

He took her hand, and they walked to the door.

"There they go, Lord and Lady Tewkbury." Robert's voice broke the silence. He scrambled to his feet. "I'm surprised you married her at all, my lord. She hasn't told you, has she?"

Edmund stopped and turned, while Ellen stood by helplessly, watching the fiasco unfold.

"Of course she hasn't. She's got you caught up in her web of lies and deceit. Not just you, Tewkbury. All of you." He turned to his audience.

"You are making serious accusations against one of my guests, Mattick. I won't have that." Dobberham's forehead glistened with sweat.

"Pray, elaborate. What do you mean?" Lady Cynthia's eyes widened in mock horror.

"Let's go. Don't listen to him." Ellen tugged at Edmund's arm.

But Edmund had turned to Robert with a snarl. "Yes, please tell us what you mean, so I can run you through with my foil."

Robert pointed a finger at her. "She's not who she says she is. Miss Ellen Robinson, the prim and proper schoolmistress, claims that her stepfather is Jacob Robinson, the famous author and poet. She has even taken his name. It's a fine Banbury tale indeed. You all believed it, didn't you?"

All eyes shifted from Robert to Ellen. She felt their glances hit her like stinging, fiery arrows.

Ellen felt a chasm open before her and wished she could throw herself into it.

"She's neither prim nor proper, and her name isn't Miss Ellen Robinson, because her father, step or otherwise, isn't Jacob Robinson."

"Oh dear," said Lady Cynthia happily.

"The lady before you is Mary-Ellen Gordon, the infamous daughter of the sixth Viscount Blackshurst." Robert shrugged. "She's considered soiled goods, although I suppose that doesn't matter now that she's established herself with Tewkbury to cover it all up. I was once engaged to her, but decided to call it off when I found out about her sordid past."

A scream ripped through the room. Ellen hardly recognised her own voice. "Liar!" She would have thrown herself at him to gouge his eyes out, but someone held her back.

"Not another word out of your lying mouth." Edmund stalked over to Robert and jabbed a finger into his chest. "We'll settle this honourably, like men." His voice was icy.

Robert shrugged nonchalantly. "If you insist. Name the terms."

"Epées without blunted tips. In the ballroom. Now." He led the way.

"This is not at all proper for the ladies," Dobberham protested as everyone followed them into the ballroom. "Lady Elinor! Think of your charge! This is not for the faint of heart."

Lady Elinor pushed her metal-rimmed glasses up her

thin nose. "Nonsense. I've always wanted to see a duel," she announced. "I wouldn't miss it for the world."

The other ladies agreed.

So it was that Edmund and Robert fought a duel in the Dobberham ballroom before an audience of ladies and their chaperones.

"To the death," Edmund growled, lifting his épée.

"No, no, no!" Dobberham interjected with a panicked expression on his face. "Don't want any corpses in my ballroom, mind you! Winner is the one who first draws blood. I shall be the referee."

THE TWO MEN WERE LOCKED IN A FIERCE, SAVAGE DANCE. They lunged and parried, twisting and turning mid-air to avoid hits. Both had shed their coats and were fighting in their shirtsleeves without masks. Sweat poured down their faces as their foils clashed again and again with sharp clanks as they lunged at each other with bitter determination. Robert was shorter and stockier and fought with unpredictable aggression, a confident smirk on his face as he returned each blow with clever feints and ripostes.

Ellen was terrified for Edmund, who escaped several stabs by a hair's breadth. What would she do if Edmund was hit, or worse, killed?

She would never forgive herself, and she could never live with the guilt of having brought him to this. She could barely watch the match.

So she barely registered that Edmund, who was taller and leaner than Robert, fenced with more methodical precision, his blows landing with elegant but deadly accuracy.

It soon became clear that Edmund was the more gifted fencer. Finally, with a decisive, swift move, Edmund thrusted the tip of his blade into his opponent's shoulder.

Robert stumbled and fell onto his back. His shirt was stained red.

It was a hit.

"Take it back," Edmund growled. "What you said about my wife."

"I can't." Robert's chest heaved.

"The truth." Edmund dug the blade in further as Robert writhed.

"The truth?" he gasped. "It *is* the truth. She is Mary-Ellen Gordon. Except I may have exaggerated a little."

Edmund nudged further. "Speak."

"She was an innocent. Does that satisfy you? Now remove your blade."

"I want the whole truth." Edmund removed the blade but kept a booted foot on his chest.

"She is Blackshurst's daughter. I met her when she was a chit, barely out of school. Her first Season." Robert's words came in short, chopped gasps. "I proposed an elopement to Gretna Green. She agreed. Blackshurst sent runners from Bow Street to intercept us halfway." He shrugged. "That's all there is to it."

"Is it true?" Edmund's eyes sought Ellen's as she stood by the window, both hands clenched over her mouth. She dropped them to her sides.

Robert hadn't mentioned that she'd changed her mind about eloping in that squalid little inn halfway to Scotland, but he'd told her it had been too late. He hadn't mentioned that he'd tried to force himself on her in that dodgy room in the inn and that she'd bitten him to defend herself. He hadn't mentioned that he'd told her he thought she was a spoilsport and that she might as well get on with it, that he'd never intended to marry her, and from now on no one would, and that her reputation would be irreparably damaged, he'd see to that.

She didn't mention that her father had been so shocked by their elopement that he'd had a heart attack and died that night.

Her heart was broken twice.

The scandal that followed was beyond anything she'd ever imagined.

Robert hadn't mentioned any of it, but perhaps that was for the best, for not everyone needed to know the sordid details.

Ellen felt an icy lump in her throat. He'd been right about one thing: she'd been soiled goods ever since.

Incapable of loving and being loved.

Incapable of experiencing a genuine marriage. This sham, this pretence in which she found herself now, was the closest to a marriage she would ever experience. It was all she deserved.

So she felt herself nod. "It's true."

ROBERT MATTICK LEFT AS SOON AS HIS WOUND WAS dressed. It turned out to be a mere scratch, even though it bled through the shirt and looked dramatic.

The men slapped Edmund on the shoulders and the ladies celebrated him as a hero when he felt anything but.

He felt weary and hollow.

Later, back in the room with Ellen, Edmund asked, "Why Robinson?"

Of all the things he could have asked, the only thing he was truly curious about was why she'd chosen Jacob Robinson as her stepfather.

Ellen sighed wearily. "Sit down," she said after the servants left the room.

He sat across from her, his head resting on his hands, and waited.

She leaned her head back against the armchair and closed her eyes as she recollected her thoughts. Then she told him what had really happened with Mattick.

"Father died that night." Her voice broke. She cleared her throat and swallowed before continuing. "The shock of seeing his only daughter elope with a man he considered unsuitable was too much for him. I was suddenly alone in the world, barely seventeen, with a scandalous reputation that society would never forgive. I immediately became a pariah. I had no one to guide me, to protect me, to tell me what to do. A very distant cousin had inherited my father's title, and he'd made clear that he didn't want me in the house. That I'd sullied the family name, and that he didn't want me near his wife in case my soiled reputation rubbed off on her by association. My former seamstress, Jenny, had married a few months earlier, a man who was much older than her, so I went to her. She'd always been more than just a seamstress; we'd become friends over time, and I trusted her. The Robinsons took me in when everyone else refused me."

Ellen's eyes filled with tears as she remembered the quiet embrace with which Jenny, big with child, had greeted her. She'd stayed with the Robinsons for two years. No one had known where she was, no one had cared, no one had ever asked for her or wondered where she'd gone. Miss Mary-Ellen Gordon had simply disappeared from society, and no one had bothered to find out what had happened to her.

The Robinsons had become a second family to her. Jacob had told her to consider him a second father, and she had done so. Ellen had helped with their baby after it was born, and Jacob Robinson had kept her busy with his manuscripts that needed to be copied in neat handwriting. It was the perfect job for her because it had kept her from thinking.

Then one day, Jacob had showed her an advertisement in *The Times*. A seminary for young ladies in Bath was looking for teachers. Jacob had gently suggested that she apply, as she fit the requirements perfectly.

Ellen had been reluctant at first. The thought of venturing out into a cold, judgmental world had frightened her. Then she'd plucked up all her courage and got on the next mail coach to Bath.

Miss Hilversham had taken one look at her and hired her on the spot. In all the years she had worked for Miss Hilversham, she had never asked about Ellen's past. Ellen had sometimes wondered if Miss Hilversham had suspected that she'd tried to hide a scandalous past, but if she had, she'd never shown it. So it came that Ellen had found her second home in the seminary.

Having sworn off marriage and love forever, she'd thought it only natural that she should follow in Miss Hilversham's footsteps and become the next headmistress. She'd looked forward to the challenge. She sent half her earnings to the Robinsons, despite Jacob's protests that he could look after his own family, thank you very much. Jenny, however, gratefully accepted the financial support.

"Men's pride," she'd told Ellen. "But I have five mouths to feed and, brilliant as Robinson is, he is not a good accountant, and money is always tight."

It'd been so easy for Ellen to forget her past. Her new life blossomed and she'd been certain that teaching was what she would do for the rest of her life. But then, one morning, Noni stood at the door...

Ellen raised a tired hand. "You know what happened next."

Edmund had listened quietly. He lifted his head and stretched his leg.

"Your past doesn't matter to me," he said. "We all have one. You've learned of mine. You would not believe what some of Dobberham's guests have to hide, including some ladies. But what Mattick has done to you is unforgivable. He took advantage of an innocent. He knew what he was doing and what the consequences would be for you. He never intended to marry you. I'd hazard a guess you were not his only victim, either."

Ellen took his hand in hers. "I know I asked you not to duel with him. But when you did, and he lay on the ground, panting and whimpering from the scratch you'd given him, I couldn't help but feel vindicated. He deserved it and more. And for that, I want to thank you."

She leaned forward and kissed him. She had intended it to be a quick peck on the lips, but she could not tear herself away. His arms pulled her towards him, and his lips roved lazily over hers. His lips were so soft that she felt butterflies fluttering all over her body. She felt something irresistible rush through her veins, a firework of emotions followed by an aching pull, a longing...

For what?

He lifted her and placed her on the bed. He kissed her neck, behind her ear, the tender hollow between her collarbones. His lips travelled upward again and nibbled on the lobe of her ears.

"Tell me to go," he said thickly. "Tell me to leave quickly."

She pulled him back. "Stay," she heard herself say. "I want you to stay."

He buried his head in her golden red locks and inhaled deeply. Then, after a long moment, he untangled himself gently and removed himself from the bed.

Ellen had her eyes pressed shut, and only by hearing the gentle click of the door did she realise he had left.

CHAPTER TWENTY-ONE

*E*verything was for the best.

Ellen tried to talk herself into believing that as Annie pulled the curtains aside and allowed the light to flood into the room. As the memories of the previous night burned in her mind, she buried her face in her pillow and groaned. She hadn't really begged him to stay, had she?

What on earth had possessed her?

Ellen no longer understood herself. She'd always been logical, cool, and practical. She'd sworn she'd never let her passions get the better of her, sworn she'd never allow herself to fall in love with a man again, not after Robert had so grossly betrayed her and ruined her life. Men could not be trusted, and the only person she could ever truly rely on was herself. That had been her credo in life, and it had served her well.

And here she was, throwing it all away.

Even for a most unsuitable man! For heaven's sake: he

was a fop, a nitwit, a nincompoop. Was she out of her mind?

And yet she'd wanted him to stay.

Because he was not the usual man. He was sensitive and kind and he had a wonderful sense of humour. He had integrity.

He had called out the man who had ruined her and almost killed him. The fop had turned into her champion; the nitwit had transformed into her knight in shining armour, who with considerable courage and strength had publicly defended her virtue.

The rebellious part of her insisted she could fight her own battles. She did not believe in knights in shining armour, and she did not want a man to save her. But realistically, she could never have picked up the foil and fenced with Robert, however much she might have wanted to. She wouldn't even have known how to hold the thing.

Perhaps she could take fencing lessons. She could ask Edmund.... but no.

Within the confines of this ridiculous sham of a marriage, he had always treated her with respect. He'd never taken advantage of the situation. Not even when she'd thrown herself at him, begging him to stay...

What on earth did he think of her now?

He'd probably think she was every bit the strumpet Robert made her out to be.

She covered her burning cheeks with her hands and wished she could stay in bed all day, with the curtains drawn. But here was Annie, cheerfully announcing that it was time to pack, for his lordship had announced that they were leaving that morning.

She got up, dressed, and dragged herself downstairs for breakfast.

He was already there, standing by the sideboard, talking to Dobberham. Pale and hollow-eyed, he hadn't slept—where would he have slept, anyway? He looked up when she came in, gave her a quick nod, then returned to conversing with Dobberham.

The dining room fell silent, and Louise rose from her seat, took her hands and led her to the breakfast table.

"We are so sorry to see you go," she chirped, "just when things were getting so exciting! This has been the most interesting house party we have ever had. Nothing can or will ever top it. What do you say, Dobberham? Isn't it a pity Lord and Lady Tewkbury are leaving?"

"Yes, my love, 'tis a great shame indeed." Lowering his voice to Edmund, he said, "But I don't blame you in the least."

Ellen noticed at once that they treated her differently.

Now that she was a Viscount's daughter, even with her reputation in tatters, she was of quality and considered a 'real' lady by those who had considered her some dreadful bourgeois schoolmistress with dangerously progressive ideas.

Oh, the hypocrisy of people!

Ellen would have laughed if she hadn't been so exhausted.

She had a simple breakfast with plain toast and weak tea.

Robert had left last night. The wound had only been a scratch, and he was quite well, but it would be a lesson. Ellen hoped she would never have to see him again.

"I cannot imagine him showing his face in society

again, not after this," Lady Dobberham said with satisfaction.

"And I can?" Ellen looked around and saw some averted faces, some puzzled, some regretful.

"Of course you can." Lady Eleanor's osprey feather in her headwear bobbed up and down as she bit into a crumpet with gusto. "It's an old story, and I daresay everyone has forgotten it. And those who haven't, like me, for I remember the scandal sheets well, won't mind now that you're respectably married to Tewkbury."

Ellen swallowed painfully.

"But of course nothing is taken for granted in the *ton*. One would have to still work at resuscitating your reputation officially. Rest assured that I shall speak only the best of Lady Tewkbury," Lady Gosford said graciously.

"Thank you," Ellen whispered.

"And it wouldn't hurt to be invited to a ball by the Duchess of Ashmore. Ashmore is the one you want on your side. Once Ashmore has smiled benignly at you, your social position is guaranteed for life."

"Then I am indeed fortunate, for the Duchess is a former pupil of mine," Ellen said.

The table erupted in delighted chatter.

Lady Gosford beamed at Ellen and patted her hand. "Well then, what are you worried about? You will see, people high and low will scramble to meet you."

Ellen smiled weakly.

She'd never been so relieved to leave a house, even though she felt sorry for Louise, who truly regretted their departure.

"I shall call on you in London, Ellen." Louise looked

determined. "We shall go shopping together and have ices at Gunter's."

Ellen felt she answered honestly when she said, "I look forward to that."

ELLEN LOOKED AT EDMUND, WHO SAT ACROSS FROM HER IN the carriage, and saw that he was asleep already, although they'd barely left the estate. His head was thrown back, his eyes closed. Next to him sat Noni. The child had been listless the past few days; the nurse had said, and he'd been coughing, but surely it was a mere cold.

His little dark head leaned against his arm, his fingers intertwined with Edmund's. Her heart squeezed.

Two men, one small and one large. How could they crawl into her heart in such a short time?

Then it hit her like a thunderbolt.

She hadn't fallen in love, had she?

Not only with one, but with both?

Good heavens!

The thought disturbed her so much that it took her breath away.

Then a ray of sunlight shone through the carriage window, illuminating Noni's face, and she saw that his little face was sickly pale.

"Stop the carriage at once."

"What?" Edmund blinked at her sleepily.

"Noni." She pulled the child away from him and onto her lap, placing her hand on his forehead. It was dry but burning hot. "The child is burning up with fever."

She'd mistaken his listlessness for the usual tiredness that came with a carriage ride, coupled with the slight cold the nurse thought he might have. She'd been too busy with her own thoughts, her own worries and troubles, and here was the child, right in front of her, seriously ill, and she hadn't noticed.

Ellen cursed herself.

"We can't possibly travel with an ill child."

"We can't?" Edmund blinked at her, confused, then hastily changed his answer when she scowled at him. "So you say. We can't."

"We can't go back to Dunworthy Manor either," Ellen fretted.

"Can't we? No. I suppose we can't." He cleared his throat.

"Edmund. Do something," Ellen pleaded. The child had begun to whimper in her arms.

Edmund shook himself, then opened the carriage window. "There's been a change of plans," he called to the coachman. "The child is ill. Take the next turn for Penwick Park. Send a rider ahead first. They need to be informed of our arrival, I suppose."

Ellen looked at him with wide eyes. "Penwick Park?"

He nodded briefly.

Ellen looked at him gratefully. "Thank you."

"Lord help me," she thought she heard Edmund murmur as the carriage turned into a wide lane leading up to the grand manor house.

CHAPTER TWENTY-TWO

*E*dmund closed his eyes, praying he'd not just made a monumental mistake.

It was too late. His mother came hurrying towards them long before their carriage reached the house. Behind her emerged the tall figure of a gentleman, who remained standing by the door.

He gulped.

"Edmund!" His mother moved to embrace him, but Edmund extended a hand to keep her at a distance. She stopped with a stricken expression on her face.

"Forgive the intrusion, but we come with an unwanted companion: some childhood illness that may very well be contagious." He turned to help Ellen lift Noni out of the carriage.

His mother stepped toward him with determination, purposefully misunderstanding him. "I'll not bid you welcome in your own home, son, where you will never be an intrusion. And there are no unwanted companions or guests. Even if they come with an illness." She stepped up to Ellen and looked at the child. "Poor little mite. We shall call the doctor immediately."

Seeing Ellen struggle with Noni's weight, Edmund lifted the child out of her arms and carried him easily up the stairs.

Where his brother waited.

IT WAS CERTAINLY STRANGE, EDMUND THOUGHT WEARILY afterwards, as Edward, his twin brother, poured him a glass of brandy. Here they were, talking politely in the very drawing room where they'd fought so bitterly a decade earlier, his brother playing host in a house that was actually his.

"Drink." Edward handed him the glass. "I think you need it."

He certainly did. He downed the glass in one gulp.

His brother stood by the fire with his arms crossed. They did not look alike, Edward and he, for they were not identical twins. Edward's hair was lighter and was receding at the hairline. He also had blue eyes, whereas his own were brown; and he was slightly shorter. Edward was the spitting image of his father, whose portrait hung on the wall above the fireplace. They had the same eagle's nose, the same proud chin.

Edward wore the plain, sober clothes of the country squire, whereas he looked like a parrot next to him.

Edmund curled his lips into a thin line and looked away from his father's portrait.

"I say. You've grown into a middle-aged squire," he tried to joke weakly, and for the life of him he could think of nothing more constructive to say.

The corners of Edward's lips turned up. "And you've grown into a hothouse flower, I see. A real tulip."

"I'm married."

"So am I."

The two brothers studied each other.

For the first time, Edmund felt uncomfortable in his pistachio trousers, orange and burgundy-striped waistcoat.

"And the boy, Mama says, is not really your child, but your ward?" asked Edward.

"Yes." It was too complicated to explain the circumstances of how he'd ended up with Noni.

"I see."

Silence.

"And you? Any children?"

Edward shook his head. "Not yet. Hopefully, Mary-Anne and I will be blessed with a child soon."

Edmund, who'd been pouring himself a second glass of brandy, almost spilled the liquid on the table. "Mary-Anne?"

"Yes, that's my wife's name."

"I say. It's just that my wife's name is Mary-Ellen. You know. Both Marys." And they'd been married about the same time, his mother had said. What a strange coincidence.

"Mary-Anne is with her parents now because her father is ill. She was due to return within the next few days, but if the boy has an infectious childhood disease, it might be better for her to stay away."

Edmund nodded.

There was silence again.

Well, dash it. He had better things to do than sit around awkwardly talking to his brother.

Edmund stood up. "I suppose I'll be retiring..."

"Why didn't you come?" Edward interrupted.

"Come where?"

"Father's funeral."

Edmund stared at the porcelain horseman on the mantelpiece that he'd loved to play with as a child.

He shrugged. "Because."

"Because." Edward's voice was flat. "Is that all you have to say? We waited for you and delayed the funeral as long as we could, but then we had to go ahead without you. Mother was heartbroken and waited and waited for you. But you never came."

"And you know very well why." Edmund's face hardened. "I am not interested in dwelling on the past, going through it all again; who said what to whom and why. I have moved on, as have you." He went to the door.

"Ned—"

Edmund stopped and shook his head. "Let's leave it at that. I am here because the child is ill, and my wife has asked me to do something about it. As soon as he is better, we will leave, and you will be able to resume your lives here, undisturbed by my presence."

He left, his heart pounding.

He'd had nightmares about his father's funeral for months. A small crowd had gathered in the cemetery of the local church. It had been pouring. And it had not occurred to anyone that the shadowy figure under the chestnut tree had been him.

He'd arrived late and had left again before anyone had recognised him.

CHAPTER TWENTY-THREE

*I*t was measles.

Fever, malaise, cough, inflammation of the eyes.

"The spots will come soon, most likely tomorrow or the day after," the doctor explained as he packed his bag. "I recommend willow bark tea to bring down the fever. A hot mustard and oatmeal poultice for the chest. And isolation. No contact with anyone in the household who hasn't had it. Keep the room dark and let the illness run its course."

Honoria, the Dowager Lady Tewkbury, said, "We've all had it; that is Edward and Edmund and myself. I dare say most of the staff have had it too, but it is well to be cautious and keep contact to a minimum."

"I've had measles too. I'll stay with the child," Ellen told Edmund's mother.

"I'll have a tray of tea brought up to you." She laid a hand on Ellen's arm. "It was right for you to come. Sad, of course, given the circumstances. But I can only be grateful that you are here."

The child was still burning with fever. Ellen wrung out the washcloth, wiped his face, and placed it on his forehead. Noni thrashed about and ripped the cloth off, flinging it to the ground.

Ellen stared at the small, writhing body, and her eyes glazed over. Measles killed children.

It had killed Emma.

Her younger sister had died of measles. It had been so long ago, but Ellen remembered it as if it had been yesterday. They'd shared a bed and had the measles together. But while she had only had a mild case, Emma had burned up with fever. By the seventh day, she had recovered, and Emma was dead.

The pain, the gnawing hole, the emptiness of losing her sister, had remained in her heart ever since.

She looked down at Noni, and a tear ran down her cheek.

She would not let this little one die. She would fight for him with everything she had.

She clasped the child's small hand and rested her head on her arm.

She was tired. So tired.

A SHARP, SWEET SCENT ENTERED HER NOSE. PUNGENT, BUT not unpleasant. It wasn't exactly mint, more like rosemary, but sharper and more pungent. Ellen lifted her head, sniffing. She didn't recognise the scent, but it was soothing, clearing her nostrils and her head.

Noni was still asleep; he had stopped thrashing around and was sleeping with his mouth half open.

A movement caught her attention.

Was she dreaming? She dreamed that an exotic prince stood at the window in a magnificent, oriental-looking banyan, scarlet and gold. His hair curled in his nape and his profile was classically handsome.

Ellen blinked dreamily at him.

He was standing at the table by the window, lifting a vial. On the table was some sort of device, a small glass lamp with a bowl over a candle, which seemed to be the source of the smell.

Edmund. Ellen snapped awake. What was he doing in Noni's room?

"What is that?" Her voice was thick with sleep. She cleared her throat.

"This is the oil from the leaves of a tree that grows in New South Wales. It is said to have healing properties." He dropped three drops of the oil into a bowl of water, dipped a cloth in it and wrung it out. Then he walked over to the child and placed it on his feverish forehead.

Ellen sniffed. "It smells nice."

"I distilled it myself. Apparently, it works against fever." He pulled out a small pouch, opened it, pulled out a leaf, and handed it to her.

It was narrow and silvery, unlike any leaf she'd ever seen before. The scent emanated from it.

"You are a connoisseur of scents," Ellen said suddenly, dazed. "I don't know why I didn't notice it before. But you have an excellent nose, and you know how to distil oils. Oh!" Her eyes widened. "I remember how the ladies used to rave about a certain perfume. Adonis."

He pulled a chair up to the bed and sat down, staring at the child. "Yes."

"You created it."

"Yes." A slight smile played on his lips.

"But that means you are a respected perfumer! You're famous!"

He shrugged. "Adonis is famous. I prefer to remain anonymous, and that people do not know who its creator is."

"But why?"

Again, he shrugged. "I prefer it that way. I have got a laboratory in Jermyn Street where I work. And I sell my perfume to the chemists and perfumers of London. Few know they are dealing with Lord Tewkbury." He stared absently into the air. "My father would have had an apoplexy if he'd known that his son dirtied his fingers doing a tradesman's work."

Ellen leaned forward. "What happened to put you at such odds with your father and brother?" He would probably withdraw again, chiding her for meddling in a business that was not her own.

But he sat in silence, thinking. Then he spoke.

His father never got over the disappointment that he not only stuttered but also had learning difficulties and couldn't read. When they resorted to punishment, it got worse. He was sent home from Harrow in disgrace after only a few weeks. His brother Edward, however, had always learned easily. By the age of five, he was reading fluently and doing sums in his head.

His father had ranted, "How can my eldest son and heir inherit my property and fortune if he is too dim-witted to read letters, sign documents and check the ledgers to see if the sums add up? All and sundry will try to outwit you and trick you with their crafty miscalculations, draining our fortune over the course of time. It will be our ruin!"

"I could do the ledgers," Edward had piped up. He was only eight.

Lord Tewkbury's face had softened. "I know you could, clever boy."

And so it had been Edward he'd invited into his office to show him the ledgers and other important documents. It had been Edward who'd learned how to run the estate. It had been Edward whom his father had wished to be heir to his title and estate, and not him.

Edmund had been left to roam the woods with Dunstan, now Lord Dobberham, gathering flowers and attempting his first distillation of violets. His father had thought that an effeminate pastime and forbidden it. When his father caught him sorting his mother's shawls to admire the fabric, he'd been grounded for a week.

Then, when he and Edward both turned sixteen, it was Edward whom his father took to London to meet the bankers and lawyers.

Edmund had stayed at home, hurt and resentful. What he wouldn't have given to go to London! He'd been burning to get to know the city and its fashions. But here he was, kicking his boots in the country.

The butler had brought him a letter that needed answering urgently.

Edmund had taken the letter into his father's office, placed it on the desk, sat down in the chair behind it and stared at it for a good half hour before deciding to open it.

It had taken him another painstaking half an hour to

decipher that it was from one of the tenants, asking for an extension on the rent.

This was his chance, Edmund thought, to prove to his father that he was as capable of running the estate as much as Edward. If he could read and reply to this letter in legible handwriting, if he could settle this business before his father and brother returned from London, then he would prove that he was indeed a worthy son and heir.

Perhaps his father would be proud of him for a change. And he would have shown that he wasn't the fool he was thought to be.

No sooner said than done, Edmund dipped the quill into the inkwell and drew letters on the paper. Dear Mr Matkin...

He'd gone through ten sheets of paper before he produced a letter that was free of mistakes and stains. He then folded the letter, wrote the name of the addressee on it and instructed a footman to deliver it to Mr Matkin immediately.

Edmund was pleased with himself and so proud that he'd been able to do this on his own and without a tutor tapping his knuckles with a ruler.

His father and brother returned after a few days, with Edward wearing a set of brand-new clothes that made Edmund jealous.

"How was it?" he'd asked his brother, who'd shrugged.

"I dare say city life is not for you," Edward said breezily. "Too noisy and smelly."

How Edmund would have loved to see London, even with all the noise and smells!

When his father called him into his study, he

wondered how he could tell his father that he, too, would like to visit London one day.

His father was standing in the middle of the study, red as a beetroot. In front of him stood a farmer, turning his battered hat in his hand and thanking him profusely.

"I shall be forever grateful," he said, shaking his hand heartily and leaving.

"What is the meaning of this?" his father had shouted, waving the letter Edmund had written.

Edmund swallowed. "It was an urgent letter from Mr Matkin. I had the matter settled to your satisfaction."

"Mr Matkin? Mr *Matkin*?" His father's eyes almost popped out of his head. "Where, in all that is good and holy, does it say Mr Matkin?"

A sick feeling settled in Edmund's stomach. He did not reply.

"I seem to recall that a certain Mr Watkins has applied for a deferment of rent, which I've already granted twice. And here comes Farmer Matkin, muddying the floor of my study, thanking me for waiving his rent for the year? Are you out of your mind?"

Edmund had confused the letters M and W.

"Matkin and Watkins, the names are so similar," he'd stammered.

"Nonsense! If you can't tell your tenants apart, you're not a worthy keeper of my land. And you want to inherit my title? You are a simpleton. A disgrace!"

"I d-d-don't want your title, sir," he'd replied, cursing himself that his stutter had returned now. "I don't want your l-l-land. You can give it all to Edward." He turned on his heel and marched to the door.

"Stop!" his father yelled. "Where do you think you're going?"

He'd closed his eyes. When he'd opened them, there was determination in them. "To L-London. And I'm not coming back. Ever."

Edward had tried to prevent him from leaving. The vicious row that had followed had shaken him to the core.

He'd left within the hour.

ELLEN LOOKED AT HIM WITH SYMPATHY IN HER EYES. "AND your mother?"

He stared at the pattern on the blanket. "Too scared of him. Never dared stand up for me. Always made excuses for him."

"I'm so sorry," Ellen whispered.

"It was for the best. I dare say I did well on my own. Made my way in the city. Started my perfumery business and created Adonis, and it flourished."

Ellen nodded. "It must have been painful to lose your family like that. You were sixteen?"

He shrugged. "Turns out I did better on my own without my family breathing down my neck all the time."

"My family disowned me too when I ran off with Robert," she heard herself say. "That is, my biological, extended family. My mother had died when I was born, and my father didn't survive the shock of my elopement." She fiddled with the fringes of her shawl. Then her face hardened. "I have got aunts and uncles who turned away from me when I needed them most." Her voice softened. "But I found my real family in the Robinsons. I would do anything for them."

"Including entering into a sham marriage with an unsuitable baron to get the son out of debtor's prison." He folded his arms behind his head.

"Yes. I never thanked you properly for that, did I? For helping Drake. For helping me, for defending my honour in the duel."

He waved it away. "I say we speak no more of the duel. It is in the past and none of it matters." He thought. "Except Robert Mattick, I say. If he dares to cross your path again, I shall have to fight him to the death."

Noni murmured in his sleep.

"Why don't you get some sleep? You must be exhausted." His eyes were on her.

"I can't just leave the child." Ellen wiped his forehead anew.

"I'll stay with him."

"But..."

"I'll wake you if there is any change. But I dare say he will sleep now. You are of no use to anyone if you are overcome with fatigue in the morning." His manner was calm and commanding.

Ellen looked at him with wide eyes. Was this the superficial dandy who seemed afraid of children? He'd fought for her. He cared for the child. He seemed like a different person since they were married.

"You like Noni." The words escaped from her mouth.

"Like?" He raised an eyebrow. "I say that's too strong a word. But I admit, the little fellow has grown on one, and one would not want to see him suffer."

"Wake me if there is any change." Ellen gave him a last look before she left.

He nodded.

Ellen slept through the night, the sleep of the weary. When she woke, the grey rays of morning crept through the window. She'd fallen on the bed with her clothes on, so she scrambled up, quickly washed her face and hurried into Noni's room.

Edmund was sitting in an armchair with his arms crossed and seemed to be dozing. The room still smelled wonderful and there were a number of small vials on the table.

His eyes opened as she approached the bed.

"The fever's broken," he said when he saw her.

Noni was asleep, his face covered with spots, his forehead wet with sweat.

"Thank you for staying with him all night. The nurse can take over the next shift."

Edmund got up and stretched.

The scarlet robe flowed around him and suited him so much better than the colourful padded vests he usually wore.

"I say. This little fellow will be well soon," he said.

"Thank you," Ellen whispered.

Edmund lifted his hand and brushed a lock of hair out of her face. "Everything will be well," he repeated.

Ellen knew he wasn't just talking about Noni.

She took his hand in hers and turned it. With her index finger, she gently drew the letter A into his palm.

He inhaled sharply.

"This is the letter A." Then she drew all the letters of the alphabet into his palm.

His breath had quickened.

He pulled his hand back and clenched it into a fist.

"I can teach you, if you want," she whispered.

He stepped back and left the room quietly.

Ellen looked after him with a squeeze in her heart.

CHAPTER TWENTY-FOUR

*N*oni's illness, fortunately, wasn't severe, and the doctor said he would recover soon.

In the meantime, they had to wait. It was odd for Edmund to be back at Penwick Park after all this time. Everything was familiar, yet strange to him. So much had changed; yet what had changed the most was himself. He'd grown up. He saw everything through fresh eyes; how efficiently his brother cared for the estate, and how lovingly his mother managed the house and the flower gardens.

Ellen loved to walk in the magnificent gardens, where the shrubs were trimmed into neat geometric shapes. Sometimes Edmund would accompany her, and they'd walk in silence, or he'd tell her stories about growing up in Penwick Park. She'd throw her head back and laugh, lightening his heart. Edmund wanted her to laugh more. He wanted to see her mouth curl into a smile, her eyes light up, her head tossed back to reveal a long, creamy throat. He wanted to plant a series of light kisses along that throat, down to the delicious little dent between her collarbones and then further down…

They no longer shared a room here at Penwick Park, and he had not visited her in her chambers. He realised with a pang that he missed the room at Dobberham Mansion, where they'd been thrown together.

He missed her, even though she was standing right in front of him.

Unbearable if she were to leave.

Unbearable if he ever lost her.

Desire and confusion rushed through him.

He pulled his arm away from her hand as he interrupted her mid-sentence. "I must go."

He felt her confused gaze between his shoulder blades as he strode away.

HE WAS AVOIDING HER, AND SHE WISHED SHE KNEW WHY.

Ellen sighed as she plucked a daisy from the ground and stared at it sadly. She thought they'd made good ground, getting closer to each other. Sometimes there were moments when she thought she was sure she meant something to him. She sometimes caught him watching her with a strange, intense look in his eyes, only to look away quickly when she met his gaze. Or the other day, when he'd tucked a strand of her hair back and his hand had brushed across her cheek, and she'd had to use all her willpower not to turn her head and plant a kiss on his palm. She'd used the trick she'd used with Noni, writing the letters of the alphabet on his palm and offering once more to teach him. Then he'd taken a step back, aloofness enveloping him like a cloak, and she felt she must have imagined it all.

What was happening? Where were they going?

And what would happen after they returned to London?

Ellen stepped around the fountain and found the Dowager Baroness, Lady Honoria Tewkbury, sitting on a bench in deep thought. She looked up at the sound of Ellen's footsteps crunching in the gravel.

"I do not wish to disturb you," Ellen stammered.

Honoria shook her head. "Come, join me here."

Ellen complied.

"How is the child?" she enquired.

"Better, now that the fever is broken. The doctor says he will improve rapidly from now on."

"That is wonderful news, indeed. I am glad. I am also glad that you have married Tewkbury and that you are here." She took Ellen's hand between hers.

"I am glad to be here," Ellen said softly.

"Tell me about my son," Honoria said after a moment's silence. "You must know him better than I do by now." A small, sad smile played on her lips.

"Well." Ellen wasn't sure if that was true. "He knows quite a bit about fashion."

Honoria nodded. "Yes. He's been interested in fashion since he was young."

"And fragrances. Did you know he creates his own perfumes and is very successful at it?"

"I did not. But how excellent for Edmund, and I can so well imagine he would be successful at it."

"He has kept it a secret from most people, I believe. I hope I did not overstep by telling you about it. But I also feel you ought to know this about your son: he is very talented in the areas that interest him."

"Thank you for sharing this with me." Honoria bowed her head.

Silence fell between them. Ellen didn't know what else to say.

"I have often reproached myself for having been too weak," Honoria said after a while, "and that I should have stood up to my husband more often. He was a force of nature: a strong, choleric personality who would accept no opposition. But I also knew underneath his loud, blustering personality and his rough exterior, he meant well." Her fingers tugged nervously at her sleeve, her skirt, her shawl, and her sleeve again. "I have got no excuse for my weakness, except that I loved them all, my husband, Edmund and Edward. And I lost Edmund in the process."

Ellen pursed her lips. "I imagine that for a sensitive child as Edmund must have been, an overbearing father who ran roughshod over him, even if he meant well, must have been distressing."

"Yes. I tried to stop him from being sent to Harrow. But his father insisted it was a rite of passage that every boy had to go through to reach manhood. A kind tutor at Harrow informed me he was not doing well, that he was terribly bullied and beaten regularly. He'd stopped eating altogether, and so I insisted that he be removed from the school. It was the only time I could assert my will against my husband's. It was the only thing I could do for Edmund. But I am afraid the damage was done, and it left deep scars in him."

"And Edward?"

"He stayed at the school and did well." Lady Tewkbury

rubbed her temple. "He was such a golden child, doing everything excellently, and he was his father's favourite. Edmund knew that, of course..."

Ellen sighed.

Honoria sat up with a start. "But all that is in the past. So many unfortunate things happened that I wish I could undo now. Alas, I can't. So let's not talk about the past anymore. Tell me about yourself. I understand you were a schoolmistress before you married Edmund."

"Yes." How would Honoria take it if she knew the truth? She decided to try. "My real name is Mary-Ellen Gordon, and I am the daughter of the late Lord Blackshurst." Lady Tewkbury looked at her politely, then a dawning realisation crept across her face. "The daughter of Lord Blackshurst? Oh."

"Exactly," Ellen replied dryly. "You've heard the story?"

"But, my dear girl. The newspapers were full of it. It would have been hard not to. They said you had disappeared entirely, and then they said you might have—you know." She made a gesture with her hand.

"Killed myself? That might have been my sad fate had not the Robinsons so kindly taken me in."

"Tell me your story," Honoria requested.

Ellen did. And because Honoria was such a good listener, Ellen told her everything else.

Drake.

The unsuitable proposal.

The hasty marriage.

Afterwards, Honoria clasped her hands together in prayer and bowed her head. Then suddenly she looked up. "Why are you so sure that the marriage is not legal?"

The question startled Ellen. "Well. Because I suppose

we agreed it would not be real... because we agreed to separate when it no longer served its purpose."

"It doesn't matter what you think. What matters is how the marriage was conducted. In church, with a recognised priest, you said your vows in front of two witnesses, a contract was signed, and the announcement was made in the papers.... In the eyes of society, everything is right and proper, my dear." Ellen met Honoria's dark eyes, so like her son's. "So, from what you have told me, it appears that your marriage to my son is legal in the eyes of the law."

A cold stone settled in Ellen's stomach. "But that would be..." She could not find the word.

"Would that be so terrible? To be truly married to my son? To be a true wife to him?" She looked at Ellen with searching eyes. "Ellen, dear. I would not want any other woman to be his wife. I have seen how good you are to him. When he is with you, he seems more balanced. Self-assured. You and the child could be the family he has been looking for all this time. Since we so dismally failed at it." She hung her head.

"He wanted a family?" Ellen stammered.

"How can there be any doubt?"

Suddenly it was all too much for Ellen. She stood up. "Thank you so much for this conversation. I hope that you are right. But we will have to leave now that Noni is better."

Lady Tewkbury nodded sadly. "Yes." She looked into the distance, then again at Ellen. "I would very much like to visit you in London."

"Of course." Ellen nodded. But who knew if Ellen would still be there when she came?

THE CARRIAGE WAS READY, AND NONI WAS WRAPPED IN warm blankets. As Ellen said goodbye to Edmund's mother, Edward turned to Edmund and took him aside. Apart from their first conversation, they had spoken little during their stay at Penwick Hall, and when they had, it had always been in the company of others. Both had done their best to stay out of the other's way.

Edmund looked warily at his brother.

"There is something I wanted you to know." Edward stepped awkwardly from one foot to the other.

"Yes?"

"The other day. I was doing the accounts, and I found a mistake."

"I say, brother. It must have shaken the ground beneath you." Edmund curled his lips into a sneer.

Edward raised a hand. "Listen. It wasn't the first time, or even the second. But the third. I just want you to know that the steward mistakenly attributed the wrong amount to the wrong name. Matkin instead of Watkins. The other day, the same thing happened to me. The names are so deucedly similar. I just want you to know that this kind of mix-up can happen to anyone. Even to our steward, who is eminently trustworthy. And even to me." He hesitated. "Do you understand?"

Edmund stared at the toes of his boots and did not answer.

"And I want you to know that your land and your estate are in good hands. I'll look after them for as long as you wish. If you decide to take matters into your own hands, just say the word. But if you prefer to go to London and not have to worry about any of this, know that everything will be taken care of to the best of my ability."

Edmund found he had a strange lump in his throat.

He nodded. "I know. I wouldn't want anyone else to look after the estate." As he said the words, he knew he meant them.

Then he cleared his throat. "You will visit us in London, yes? And you must bring your wife as well."

Edward took his hand and squeezed it. "With pleasure."

Edmund said goodbye to his mother, who also promised to visit them in London soon.

It was with relief and a strange lightness that Edmund sat in the carriage as it pulled out of Penwick Park. His relationship with both his mother and brother was clearly strained, their conversations stilted, for they had been estranged for far too long. It was too much to expect that a week's stay at Penwick Hall would overcome all the resentments that had built up over a lifetime.

But something had changed. He closed his eyes and listened deep within himself. Something was definitely missing.

The sting was gone.

As the carriage left his estate, a slim, white hand crawled into his and pressed it tight.

He stared down at it and felt himself tense up again.

Ellen.

What would he do with her?

She would leave him now that the marriage had served its purpose. He knew he was an idiot; it had been drilled into him all his life. But even he had to admit that this time his idiocy had gone beyond all bounds.

What had he been thinking?

He hadn't. That was the problem.

What would they do after they returned to London?

They had two options. The first was to end the charade, pay her the rest of the money, and let her go. Make sure she was safe somewhere. He'd promised her a house somewhere in the country, with an annuity that would keep her comfortable for the rest of her life. He could not bear the thought of Ellen alone, in that dreary little house, or with anyone else.

The thought almost made him physically ill.

How on earth had he ever been so cold-blooded as to consider this a viable option? He was worse than Robert Mattick. She would be ruined for life. First, he'd publicly defended her reputation, then he'd ruin it again. And what would he tell the world? His friends? He imagined saying to his mother and brother, or even Dobberham: "Oh, we decided we didn't get on after all, so we separated."

No one would believe them.

The other option was to accept that the marriage was real.

With his luck, it might even be legal. Both were of age, they weren't related in any way, both had given their consent, there had been witnesses, it had been performed by a recognised clergyman, and they had signed all the right papers.

He mentally ticked all the boxes for a legal marriage.

Divorce wasn't an option.

An annulment?

Unlikely.

He could very well find himself married to her for life.

The thought made his mouth dry, his heart pound and his palms sweat.

Ellen bent her head and asked with a frown, "Are you feeling well?"

For one second only, Edmund thought of replying, "I have only just discovered that I worship the ground you walk on, except you can never know that, and I had better get rid of you as soon as possible before you do, and my heart will surely break when you leave."

"Just tired," he replied, and closed his eyes.

She was beautiful. Sparkling, fiery, a goddess, good-hearted, kind, and intelligent. Her scent wafted into his nose and if his eyes hadn't already been closed, he would have done so, leaning back with a sigh. He took a deep breath.

Then he wanted to bang his head against the wall of the carriage in frustration.

It was clear as daylight: he could never be a true husband to her.

Because he could never be worthy of her.

CHAPTER TWENTY-FIVE

*E*llen looked at Edmund enquiringly as the carriage pulled up to his house in Hanover Square.

"Are you sure you're well?" she asked a second time as they descended from the carriage.

"I'm fine," he replied in a clipped tone before handing his cane to the footman and striding ahead.

Ellen knitted her forehead into a worried frown. What had got into him? He'd been sullen and silent the entire trip.

Mr West greeted him inside. "I trust you had a pleasant stay, my lord. My lady." He bowed briefly.

"It was tolerable." Edmund handed his hat to Jenkins.

"There are some pressing business matters we need to discuss." Mr West hesitated, glancing at Noni, who pushed past him and scampered up the stairs, followed by the nurse. His expression softened. "Regarding the little fellow, here."

"Noni? What about Noni?" Ellen asked.

"I think it would be best if we discussed this in my office. Before you meet—Lord Tennbury." Mr West frowned.

"Tennbury? Never heard of him," Edmund said, as they stepped into Mr West's office.

"He lives across the square. I have taken the liberty of enquiring with our solicitors about the guardianship of the child." Mr West raised both hands. "There is nothing. Not a single letter, no official statement, no contract, no agreement, nothing. All we have is this." He held up the letter Noni had arrived with at Miss Hilversham's seminary. "I studied the handwriting in great detail. I am afraid I have discovered something we have all overlooked."

"What?" Edmund barked.

Mr West pulled out the letter and showed it to them. "This is not number eleven, but seventy-seven. Seventy-seven Hanover Square, which is Lord Tennbury's residence. The hook at the top of the numbers is so narrow that they can be mistaken for number ones. The writer made no distinction between the number seven and the number one, which had misled everyone.

And his signature is Tennbury, not Tewkbury. It is so similar to his Lordship's signature that I didn't notice the difference at first. I am very sorry."

"Jove's beard, West, what is the meaning of all this?" Edmund snatched the letter from his hand.

"I am afraid we have made a terrible mistake. I contacted Lord Tennbury at seventy-seven Hanover Square, and he confirmed that he had a ward called Noni whom he had sent to the seminary in Bath." Mr West looked crushed. "I'm terribly sorry, sir, but you are not

Noni's guardian, after all. And what is worse, his lordship is waiting in the drawing room to collect the child as we speak."

Ellen felt her legs buckle underneath her, and she sank into a chair. "No," she breathed.

CHAPTER TWENTY-SIX

*E*llen walked into the drawing room as if in a bad dream.

Surely she couldn't have made such a colossal, terrible, unforgivable mistake?

An elderly gentleman with a shock of white hair rose from the sofa, leaning on an ivory cane.

He had a gaunt face with thin lips and white, bushy eyebrows.

"I do not understand." His voice sounded rusty and unamused. "I sent the child to be looked after in an exclusive school in Bath, and now I am told he is here, in the neighbourhood—in this house?"

Ellen felt like dropping to the floor. Tewkbury didn't answer at all. He stood frozen, statue-like.

"There has been an unfortunate mistake," Mr West stammered.

"Then enlighten me!" the man boomed.

"Forgive us, Your Lordship, but first we need to confirm that Noni is indeed your ward. Could you please sign this blank piece of paper so that we can compare signatures?" Mr West held out a sheet of paper.

"What for?" Tennbury barked. "I make it a rule not to sign anything that my lawyers haven't seen."

"It's just a blank sheet of paper, and you can burn it immediately afterwards. The purpose is to compare your signature with that on the letter. It would be proof that Noni is indeed your ward. Forgive me, sir, for inconveniencing you in this way, but surely you can see that this is in the best interests of the child, for you must understand that we can't just hand him over to anyone who claims to be his ward."

Firebolts shot out of the old man's eyes. "Very well. Give it to me." He scribbled his signature on the paper. Mr West took out the letter and compared the two.

He showed it to Edmund, whose face had gone deathly pale. His eyes sought Ellen's. She took the two sheets of paper with trembling hands.

She held them up to the light and placed the newer signature over the older one.

They were identical.

Tennbury.

"I'm so, so sorry," she choked out as tears filled her eyes. She dropped onto a sofa and covered her eyes with her hands.

"I say. If anyone is responsible for this fiasco, it is me. What happens now?" Edmund's voice was tense as he turned to Mr West.

Mr West gestured at the old man, who glared at them. "It's up to him. I suppose we should call the child—"

"There's no need for that," the old man replied testily. "I have arranged for the child to be cared for in that school," he pointed his stick upwards, "so that is where he must be."

Ellen woke from the torpor that had gripped her. She pulled herself to her feet and looked at the old man with irritation. "No, that's not at all where he needs to be."

"Young woman, I do not know who you are and why you speak to me in that tone," the old man replied haughtily.

"Look out, Tennbury, you're talking to my wife," growled Edmund.

"Lady Tewkbury, then." He pulled his thin lips to a humourless smile. "If someone could enlighten me as to what is going on, I would be most grateful." He stomped his cane into the ground.

"I am Ellen Robinson. That is, I was Ellen Robinson before I married Tewkbury, here. We found Noni at Miss Hilversham's Seminary for Young Ladies, standing all alone on the porch with only a small trunk and this letter." She gestured to the letter that Mr West was still holding in his hands.

"He is with a footman," the old man grumbled. "But he had strict instructions to return as soon as the child had been deposited at the school."

"I say, your footman took those instructions a mite too literally." Edmund tapped his snuff box before opening the lid to retrieve a pinch.

"Noni was all alone!" Ellen glared at the old man. "He could not explain where he came from, for you know the child does not speak."

"Unnatural child," the old man sniffed.

"He is not unnatural!" Ellen said indignantly. "And there must be a reason why he doesn't speak. Regardless,

Miss Hilversham has decided that the child cannot stay at the seminary. I was told to return him to his guardian. As your handwriting is so illegible, I thought it said 'Hanover Square Eleven, signed Tewkbury.'"

Tennbury stared at her in disbelief. "You brought him here thinking Tewkbury was his guardian? And you," he lifted his cane at Edmund, "you swallowed that bag of moonshine and couldn't even remember whether you have a ward or not?"

Edmund coughed.

"You really are the fool you look," the old man said contemptuously.

Edmund did not deny it.

"Now, look here, sir, there is no need for insults." Mr West, bless his soul, jumped in to defend his master. "It was a misunderstanding. I, too, am at fault."

"Worse and worse. You, as his secretary. Did you not notice that this was not your master's signature?"

Mr West looked at Edmund for help.

Edmund finally spoke. "See here, it's simple. I never sign anything unless I can help it, and I never write any letters. That's why I have got a man of business to do this for me. I'd assumed it was my previous secretary who'd written the letter and that, err, I'd forgotten I'd signed it." He shrugged. "Things happen."

Tennbury snorted.

"West was hired a day before the boy arrived," Edmund continued. "So, no, he would not have known what my signature normally looks like."

The old man sniffed. "Another one of those illiterate fools who thinks they don't need to be able to read and write as long as they have one of those men to look after their affairs. It must be a modern sentiment. And you said you were a schoolmistress? For you to make such a mistake is unforgivable." He pointed his cane at Ellen.

Ellen hung her head. "It is, indeed. I shall never forgive myself."

The man fell back on the sofa with a groan. "So the child is here. What am I to do with him now?"

There was silence.

The old man sighed. "I suppose I'd better clarify something: I am not the true guardian, either."

"No?" said all three, Edmund, Ellen and Mr West at once.

The old man shook his head, and it was a wonder it didn't creak. "No. My son is the child's guardian."

"Your son." Edmund frowned.

"Captain John William Carew." The old man stared off into the distance.

Ellen, Mr West and Edmund looked at each other. Mr West shook his head, and Edmund shrugged. None of them were acquainted with Captain Carew.

"So Captain Carew was your son," Mr West chimed in helpfully. "And he is Noni's true guardian. And?"

"Was. He died in Italy four years ago." The old man roused himself from the depths of his thoughts and looked at them. "He survived the horrors of the Peninsular Wars and Waterloo, only to die of a cold in a poor street inn somewhere in Tuscany."

"I'm so very sorry," Ellen said. "That's tragic indeed."

"Yes. You see, the problem was that he had a friend, a certain Giovanni Battista, who'd served in the Royal Sicilian Foot Regiment, and in the chaos of the battlefield, he saved my son's life. A few moments later,

Battista himself was shot, and before he died, he extracted a last promise from my son: that he would take care of his newborn. The child's mother had died in childbirth. And the fool that my son was, he made that promise. So after the war, he trudged off to Tuscany to find the child. It was worse than finding a needle in a haystack, but my son was a man of his word and would keep his promise." The old man's pale, watery eyes looked at her sightlessly.

"It sounds like your son was a hero," Ellen said quietly.

"Of course he was. Got the Waterloo medal and all. But then he felt it was his duty to find the child and bring him back to England. Well, he found him. Only John fell ill and died on the way. I dare say if he'd never set foot on Italian soil to find that child, a child that's not even his, he'd still be alive today."

What was there to say? He was a bitter, grieving man, blaming a child for his son's death.

"And then?" Ellen asked breathlessly.

"He wrote me a letter before he died, begging me to find the child and take care of him. I sent my people out to find him, and it took them four bloody years to find the boy. But they found him. Had him delivered to that seminary right away."

Ellen rubbed her forehead wearily. "It's an incredible story. Both you and your son are to be commended for keeping your promises. But now we are back at the beginning. The seminary cannot take the boy. What is to be done?"

There was silence. Then the old man's voice, as tired and rusty as a creaking door hinge, said, "I dare say bring him down, and I'll have a look at him. It was my son's last wish that I care for the boy. If he kept his word, then so shall I."

Ellen's heart weighed down heavily. "May I suggest you take the nurse with you as well? He will do much better with someone he knows, and you will not have to worry about finding a suitable nurse for the child."

The old man's face brightened. "That is a practical suggestion. Then let it be done."

Noni did not shed a single tear, but Ellen was close to breaking down.

Saying goodbye to Noni was heart-wrenching and cruel. With an iron will, she pushed her feelings down and kept a cheerful disposition. The child was not to know that her heart was breaking. Noni looked at her curiously, clearly not understanding why he was expected to go with that old man.

"Lord Tennbury is your real guardian, Noni," Ellen explained as she knelt on the floor in front of him.

The child looked at her with big, serious eyes.

"We'll visit you soon, I promise." Ellen smiled weakly.

Susie, his nurse, took the child's hand, and he willingly followed her out the door.

Mr West slipped away, muttering that he had work to do.

"I'm so sorry," Ellen told Edmund for the hundredth time when they were left alone in the hall. She'd run out of words. Her eyes burned with unshed tears.

Edmund had looked at her as if he had woken from a sleep. "What exactly are you sorry for?" His voice was colder than frostbite. "For keeping your true identity a secret? For the charade of a marriage we put on? Or for making a mistake that anyone could have made?"

She choked back a sob. "No, it's not just a mistake. I should have known better, as Tennbury said. Misreading documents like that is unforgivable."

When he didn't answer, she looked up and was startled by the grim expression on his face.

"Misreading documents happens. It is regrettable, but not unpardonable. What is unpardonable is not to grant clemency for foolish mistakes, or, what is worse, to grant it too late."

Ellen blinked at him in surprise. His face was a mask, and he had withdrawn from her.

Ellen ran her dry tongue over her lips. "Maybe we could talk about this."

He shook his head. "I'd rather not. I just... I have to go. I need to go. I need to go out and think." With those words, he left her alone in the hall.

Ellen stumbled into her bedroom, dropped on the bed, and stared at the wallpaper with dry eyes.

Noni was gone.

It was all her fault. Everything that had happened had been a consequence of this first unforgivable error.

She wrapped her arms over her middle and doubled over, gasping at the intensity of the pain that had taken hold of her. She was grieving for a child that had never been hers.

Yet the tears would not come.

Not even with the realisation that she was not only grieving Noni, but so much more.

A charade of a marriage, he'd said.

That's what it had been, hadn't it? He'd promised

nothing more. She'd gone into it with the understanding that she couldn't expect more. It had been a business arrangement, and she'd accepted that.

Then why did it hurt so much?

Had she really believed they could be her new family? Edmund and Noni, and herself. She had to admit to herself that for a while she'd allowed herself to do so, indeed. Underneath the raging pain, she felt foolish for having allowed herself to dream that dream, even for a minute.

Foolish for having dared to dream of love.

She had bungled everything terribly, and now her role in all of this was clearly over.

Still, the tears would not come.

She blinked, and her hand shook as she wiped her brow.

She looked at her surroundings as if now realising where she really was.

Why on earth was she still here?

She pulled the trunk out from under the bed and threw some of her meagre belongings into it. There weren't many, as most of the clothes belonged to Lady Tewkbury, a bittersweet role she would now have to put aside. She would have to borrow the coat, for she'd given her old one away, and the pair of new boots.

She had to get away. Go home.

To Miss Hilversham's Seminary for Young Ladies.

CHAPTER TWENTY-SEVEN

*E*dmund had gone to his fencing club, where the men slapped him on the back and congratulated him on having won the fencing duel against Mattick. Rumour had spread faster than ink in water, its gossipy tendrils spreading across London until they reached every salon and drawing room. But when his friends suggested they go for a drink to celebrate, Edmund shook his head, mumbled something incoherent, and left.

In his perfume laboratory, he aimlessly mixed liquids from vials, sniffed them, wrinkled his nose in disgust and poured the concoction away. What on earth was he doing? Had he lost his sense of smell? This stuff was vile.

Then he stood with the vial in his hand, staring at the ceiling and pondering on his life.

If one came and thought of it, his bachelor life hadn't been so bad. He'd had his routine, his clothes, his perfume business, his fencing, his club. His life had been a settled routine, nothing too exciting, nothing too dramatic. Predictable but safe.

Then she'd arrived. And from one day to the next, his life had been a jumble of change, confusion and disorder. From one day to the next, he'd had a child in the house and a wife. Gone was his routine, his settled life.

People had congratulated him on his marriage with a surprised look in their eyes, as if they'd never expected him to tie the knot. When Dorington at the fencing club had said, "In the family way, I see," with an approved nod, he'd felt an odd sense of... pride.

Edmund swallowed.

Then there was her.

He'd been surprised when she'd agreed to his business arrangement, and it was an even greater surprise that they'd settled into married life so naturally, as if it had always been meant to be.

When had he forgotten they were only pretending?

Edmund scratched his neck in confusion.

He remembered how much he'd enjoyed kissing her during those silly parlour games.

Then this fellow Mattick had appeared, a man from his wife's past that he'd known nothing about, and he'd realised how little he really knew about her, and he'd been shaken out of his complacency. Every glance Mattick had thrown her had filled him with such violent jealousy it had left him nearly breathless. How dare that man touch his wife! Beating him in that duel had been the best thing he'd ever done. Edmund gritted his teeth at the thought of how Ellen must have suffered, of how she'd been socially ostracised because of the scoundrel.

She was no Miss Robinson with a bourgeois back-ground, but Mary-Ellen Gordon, the daughter of a

Viscount. When he'd told her he didn't care about her past or her reputation, it had been true, for he truly didn't care.

Then the child had fallen ill. There had been a moment, the night he'd spent alone in the bedroom with Noni, when his world had toppled, for it was then that he'd realised how much he cared for the boy. And that his heart would be badly bruised if he ever lost him—or Ellen.

Now the child was gone.

He'd never been Noni's guardian.

Edmund wondered why there was no profound sense of relief or lightness, no lifting of the weight that had been on his shoulders. If anything, it had grown heavier.

He'd reluctantly grown to like the way the boy's little eyes had lit up every time he'd entered the room, and how he'd insisted on putting his sticky, wet little hand in his and holding on to it as if it were the only thing he'd ever had in his whole life. How his eyes had turned to him in confusion, and how they'd gradually filled with tears as the old man had led him out of his house.

There had been tears in Ellen's green eyes too.

She'd wanted to talk about it, but he'd frozen, brushed her off and ran away.

Ellen. His wife.

What would happen to her now?

He would have to give her the rest of the money, as agreed in the contract, and she would disappear from his life, and everything would be right again, and he could finally return to his old lifestyle and forget that any of this had ever happened.

He wanted to smash the vial against the wall.

"I'm such a fool." He slapped his hand against his forehead.

WHEN HE REACHED HIS HOUSE, THE BUTLER LOOKED AT HIM in astonishment. "Your hat and coat, my lord?"

Edmund looked down at himself.

Oh.

He'd left the laboratory without his hat and coat, and trudged through the streets in shirtsleeves, still holding the vial.

Was that why everyone had looked at him so strangely? It had started to rain, and his hair and clothes were wet.

No matter.

He handed the vial to the butler, ran up the stairs, tore off his wet clothes, and pulled on his banyan.

"Would you like a light luncheon, my lord?" Jenkins called to him.

"Where is she?" Edmund barked in response.

Jenkins avoided his gaze. "Her ladyship has left for Bath."

"When will she return?"

"I'm not sure, sir, but it seems she left a letter in her room."

Edmund walked into her bedroom. There was a letter propped against the mantelpiece.

He cursed under his breath and tore it open.

She'd written in large, carefully crafted letters that he could painfully decipher only after they stopped dancing in front of his eyes.

I AM SO SORRY.
   Ellen

EDMUND CRUMPLED THE PAPER UP WITH A SNARL AND threw it into the fireplace. Then he dropped onto the bed, exhausted.

He listened.

The house was silent.

Any servants currently in the house were flitting about in silence, invisible.

Back to the silence and order of his bachelor days. He would have all the time in the world to devote to his perfumes and his fashion. He would no longer have to tiptoe around his own house when he returned from a night of carousing. In fact, he could now carouse as much as he liked. No one was around to care.

He left the room and went into the nursery.

The bed was made, and the toys were arranged in a box. On the bed was a stuffed bear.

He picked it up and stared at it.

"Sir?" Jenkins stood at the door. "What do you want us to do with the child's toys? Shall we donate them or have them taken to Lord Tennbury?"

His fingers clenched around the bear's fur. "Touch nothing in this room or in the room where she taught him."

"But, sir, the housemaids are already turning it back into a drawing room."

"Put everything back the way it was. Every speck of dust," Edmund growled. "I want nothing changed or moved."

SOFI LAPORTE

The butler blinked. "Very well, sir."

Clutching the child's toy, and wearing only his banyan and slippers, Edmund Graves, Sixth Baron Tewkbury, Pink of the *ton*, Exquisite, fop and gentleman of fashion, burst into Hanover Square, not caring what he looked like, for his single-minded focus was on the house across the square: number seventy-seven.

He hammered impatiently on the door.

A flustered footman opened, his eyes widening at the sight of Edmund. "S-sir."

"Where is the child?" Edmund did not wait for an answer and pushed past him into the hall.

The house was gloomy and dark, like a mausoleum. Not a fit place for a child.

Lord Tennbury stepped into the hall, looking cross. "Speak of the devil. The child tells me he has finished his visit here, that he finds my house too dark and cold and the biscuits dry, and that he wishes to return to his parents. When I asked him who his parents are, he said they are named Ned and Ellen. I suppose by Ned he must mean you." He lifted his quizzing glass to examine Edmund.

Edmund's mouth dropped. "Noni? Noni speaks?"

"I have not the faintest idea why you continue to insist that the child does not speak, when he has done nothing else since the moment he set foot here, enquiring with a repetitive stubbornness that is most tiresome, as to when he may finally return home. It does strain the nerves, I must say." The old man rubbed his temple.

Quick little footsteps approached, then a small body lunged at Edmund. He dropped the bear and threw his arms around the child.

"Noni." His lips tried to form more words, but he found himself strangely speechless as he held the child against him.

"I say. I want to go home now, Ned," said a high-pitched little voice in perfectly accented King's English, adding for politeness, "If you please."

"Noni! I say! You can speak!" Edmund dropped to his knees and looked at the child, thunderstruck.

"Can we go?" Noni tugged at his sleeve.

Edmund looked up at Tennbury. "I made a grave mistake. I should never have let him go. I have taken responsibility for this child, and I shall—no, I must—honour that responsibility. You can call in the lawyers if you want, but Noni belongs to me—and to my wife. We'll fight for the right to care for this child if necessary."

"Not so fast, young man. Nobody said anything about lawyers or a fight." Tennbury raised a thin eyebrow. "On the contrary. If you're prepared to take him off my hands, that would be the best news I've had since my son died. My promise to my son was that I would look after Noni. That does not mean I have to do it personally. I see that he has formed a close bond with you. With that in mind, I think it would be best if you formally assumed guardianship."

Edmund nodded curtly. "I intend to adopt him, sir."

The man raised his hand wearily. "Do as you please, as long as you ensure the child is kept safe and happy."

"Thank you, sir. I believe it to be in the best interests of all, the child, myself... My business man will be in touch."

The old man waved him off.

Noni tugged at his hand. "Let's go."

EDMUND STOOD OUTSIDE IN HANOVER SQUARE, LOOKING down at Noni. "Since when can you talk?"

Noni shrugged and hopped from one cobble to the other.

"Surely Ellen will know what to do," Edmund muttered.

Ellen.

A wave of panic swept through him. He opened his pocket watch. The next coach to Bath left in half an hour. He would be able to make it to Charing Cross in time.

"Noni. I'm sure you'll tell me all about it, but first I have to catch Ellen. Can you stay with Jenkins in the meantime?"

Noni nodded solemnly. "I say, I can."

Edmund stared. "Dash it, Noni. You aren't about to end up talking like me, are you?"

Noni grinned.

Edmund called for his carriage from a distance to Jenkins, who was waiting outside his door. He held out his hat and cloak.

Edmund brushed them aside. "I must go to Charing Cross at once."

As luck would have it, there was heavy traffic all along Regent Street due to an accident that had blocked the road. No matter the amount of cursing, cajoling, bribing and praying, the carriage inched its way along the road until it reached the Golden Cross Inn at Charing Cross.

Edmund jumped out of the coach and looked around wildly. It was chaos. Coach after coach was either arriving or leaving the inn. The place was crawling with horses, people and their luggage and more.

He grabbed the coachman's arm. "Where is the coach to Bath?"

"Too late. It left five minutes ago, sir," the coachman replied.

Edmund's shoulders slumped. He'd missed it.

Ellen was gone. A black void opened before him as the impact of his words sank in.

He had lost her.

ELLEN SAT ON THE STAGECOACH TO BATH, SQUEEZED between a redcoat, a young woman in a threadbare coat, a seedy-looking gentleman who reeked of alcohol, two elderly gentlemen busily discussing the politics of the day, and a woman with a basket and flyaway raven hair. She had a paisley shawl draped over her shoulders and looked familiar.

As Ellen sat next to her, the woman broke into a smile, revealing a gap between her two front teeth. "Ah, missus, we meet again!"

Ellen stared at her, perplexed.

"Henny Miller, don't ye remember? We chatted all the way from Bath to Lunnon."

So they had. It felt like decades ago.

"And where's yer little 'un?" The woman bent to look outside to see if she'd left him there. "Ye left 'im in Lunnon?"

"Oh. You mean Noni." A pain pierced Ellen's heart. She clutched her bag in her lap and looked at the woman helplessly. What on earth was she supposed to tell this woman? The truth? She was so tired of all the lies.

"E's such a right 'un, a lovely child indeed."

Ellen swallowed. "Yes."

The door opened, and another passenger squeezed in. The coach was still at the inn, but about to leave.

"Here, ye sit in me place, and I'll sit next to this lovely lady 'ere so we can chat." Henny squeezed into the seat next to Ellen and beamed at her.

"So tell me, where's yer little boy?"

Ellen stared blindly out of the window. She heard the postillion blow the horn, and the coach set in motion.

She'd left him with a cranky old man who was his true guardian, she could say. A stranger who did not want him. After she'd made the terrible mistake of leaving him with a fop of a baron who was not his guardian and had had asked her to pretend to be his wife.

Instead, she whispered wretchedly, "The child is with his guardian."

Henny looked at her sympathetically and patted her hand. "It's all well, luv. It'll work out somehow."

Ellen pulled out a handkerchief. It was Edmund's. She gave a hollow laugh and blew her nose.

"Ye love him, don't ye?" No doubt she meant Noni, which Ellen could answer in the affirmative, but Ellen's mind opened up to an entirely different possibility.

Ellen stared at her. "I-I do, actually. I love him very much. Both of them."

Then she burst into tears.

"Well, that's very good then." Henny patted her shoulder. "Then things are very simple."

"Are they?" Ellen sniffed into the handkerchief.

"Of course they are, dear. If ye love them, ye have to be with 'em."

The simple truth of that struck Ellen like a bolt of

lightning. *If you love them, then you have to be with them....*
She knocked on the carriage wall. "Let me out. Let me out! I have changed my mind. I need to get off."

The carriage rumbled to a halt, but it might have stopped anyway because a milkmaid led a cow across the road.

Ellen threw her arms around Henny's neck. "Thank you so much."

"Ye're welcome." Henny winked at her. "Now get 'im."

Ellen fought her way back to Charing Cross, between carriages, people, horses and all sorts of other animals, for it seemed all of London was out on the streets.

Home. She had to get home.

Home was Edmund and Noni; she was now certain about that now.

She stood under the brass statue of King Charles I and wondered which way to go. Where could she get a hackney?

She ran back to the inn, hoping the innkeeper would help her.

The innkeeper stood by the gate, talking to a man in a bright red banyan. The figure was tall, and dark curls fell in a familiar way across his high forehead as he gestured in frustration.

"Edmund!" She threw herself at him, catching him off-guard.

Then his arms clasped her tightly, and his face broke into a smile. "I say. There she is. My wife."

"I tried, but I can't leave. I am so sorry," she babbled. "It would be so wrong for me to return to Bath when all my heart's desire is..." she stumbled as she saw his warm eyes on her.

He stroked a strand of hair out of her face. "Is where, my love?"

"Is...is... what did you say?" The noise, the bustle of the inn and the street fell away.

"My love." He took her face in his hands. "My one and only love, I say. I realised I was being a bit of a fool, which ought to surprise no one, least of all myself. But things were moving too fast, and it was all a tad overwhelming. Then I snapped out of it and ran over to Tennbury to get Noni back. I don't know what maggot ate that part of my brain that said it was acceptable to leave the child in that man's hand for longer than a second. Turns out the old man was pretty relieved to get rid of him. I'm going to adopt Noni, you know."

Ellen gasped. "Edmund, that's wonderful!"

"Yes, and then I had another revelation, although it may be that I had this revelation before I had the other one." He lifted both fingers to gesticulate.

Ellen tipped her head to one side.

"I've been meaning to tell you ever since Dobberham Manor—well, before that. Only then one thing led to another, and we never really had time to discuss it."

"Edmund," Ellen said, "what are you talking about?"

"The thing about us being married." He drew his eyebrows together. "Not a pretend one, but the real thing. I would like that very much. Wouldn't you?" He looked at her anxiously. "Would you want to be my wife, for real? Could you really have someone like me for a husband— for real?"

"Edmund, what are you saying? Someone like you." She lifted her hands and cupped his face, tracing his eyebrows, his nose. "I couldn't imagine anyone else *but* you. You are my heart's desire."

His face broke into a smile. "Truly?"

"Truly."

They kissed in the middle of the courtyard, with carriages passing by; the smell of horse manure overpowering them and mud splattering them as the stagecoaches rattled past.

But neither Edmund nor Ellen noticed.

EPILOGUE

*T*he coach drove up the stately mansion house in Paradise Row, Bath. As Ellen descended, she clutched her husband's hands tightly.

Noni hopped down first and skipped ahead, announcing that he'd be playing in the garden.

The boy had turned into a little whirlwind of energy, and now that he'd finally found his voice, he did not stop talking.

"Like a waterfall." Edmund laughed, for the child had chatted the entire way from London to Bath. "Good that he runs off his excess steam in the garden."

A dainty, dark-haired girl wearing a housemaid's garb opened the door and curtsied.

"Is Martha gone?" Ellen asked, surprised.

"Indeed, milady. May I extend a sincere welcome to Miss Hilversham's Seminary for Young Ladies? I trust, milord, milady, that you had a good trip?" She folded her hands and looked at them expectantly, as if wanting to hold a parlour conversation.

"Er. Yes, indeed." Edmund blinked at her.

"Excellent. If you would follow me. Her Grace awaits you." She led them to the parlour with slow, measured steps, curtsied again, and left.

"Ah, Tewkbury." A tall man with a mop of dark hair drawled as he strolled into the drawing room.

"Rochford." Edmund's face brightened. "I thought you'd be here."

Ellen looked from one man to the other. "What. You two know each other?"

"Of course we do," the Duke of Rochford said. "I have often turned to Tewkbury for fashion guidance in return for advice on gambling. Though as far as I remember, gambling was never your forte, was it? I hear you have been kidnapping and marrying one of our schoolmistresses? Miss Hilversham won't be pleased." He slapped Edmund on the back with a grin. "Miss Robinson." He nodded at her. "Or should I say Lady Tewkbury, now?"

The Duchess of Rochford, more commonly known as Miss Hilversham, stepped into the room, in her arms a mewling bundle.

The words died on Ellen's lips. "What? When?"

"Last week. Meet Lady Iphigenia Marie." Miss Hilversham beamed. She was rounder, softer; her entire demeanour, dreamier. Motherhood evidently suited her.

"You must forgive me. I have received your letters, of course, but I was rather busy with this little lady, here. Rochford has had to take over the running of the school on his own, can you imagine? Instead of a headmistress, a headmaster, and not just anyone, but a duke! It is unheard of. A scandal. But we are getting used to scandals, are we not? You wouldn't believe how much our pupils are enjoying it." She looked at her husband fondly.

Rochford took the baby from her arms and cuddled her. "Lady Iphigenia is keeping us busy, indeed. And you must admit, I make a formidable headmaster. Everyone does as I say. It is most satisfying."

"Yes, but only because all the girls are in love with you." Miss Hilversham sniffed.

The raven-haired housemaid entered again. She was excessively pretty, and if she hadn't worn a housemaid's garb, one could easily have mistaken her as one of the pupils.

"Anna, get the guest room ready for his lordship and her ladyship, if you please."

"Yes, Miss Hilversham."

Ellen turned to Miss Hilversham. "A new maid? But where is Martha?"

"She resigned to take care of her ailing mother," Miss Hilversham explained. "There have been some significant changes since you were gone. But let us all have a seat."

Everyone sat, except for Rochford, who walked up and down, patting his baby on the back.

Miss Hilversham pursed her lips as she looked at Ellen. "I must say, I am most displeased."

Ellen's heart sank.

"Once I finally found the time to read your missive, I thought I must have misread it. It reads like a Banbury tale, all of it. First, delivering the poor child to the wrong guardian," her tone grew more and more severe, "then a pretend marriage to Tewkbury? Ellen! What on earth has ridden you to agree to such a scheme?"

"A pretend marriage? I've tried much in my life, but

that's one thing I must say I haven't tried." Rochford grinned.

Miss Hilversham slapped his arm, but then smiled. "Too late for that, Your Grace."

"I say, our marriage was entirely legal to begin with," Edmund interjected. "And regarding Noni, Your Grace, the blame is not to be laid on Ellen's doorstep, but on mine."

Miss Hilversham lifted a slim hand and looked at Edmund severely. "I shall get to you later, your lordship."

He swallowed.

"Your letter, Ellen, was one of the most shocking missives I have ever read," she continued. "But, I must say this, for it is true: none of it would have happened if I had just kept the child to begin with. So neither of you is to blame at all. The blame lies on my doorstep alone."

"But, Eleonore," Ellen began, startled, "You know that is not true."

"Of course it is. I don't know what I was thinking. Of course, I should have kept the child, even though he is a boy." She glanced outside the window and frowned. "The child is running towards the lake, by the by." She rang the bell for Anna and told her to send out someone to supervise the boy.

Afterwards, she continued. "My only solace is that you were with the child all the time, so he received the best care he could possibly receive. Seen in this light, it was a good decision to take on Tewkbury's dubious offer of marriage, if only for the child's welfare. No doubt you have had your own reasons, which you will tell me in your own time. As for me, I have lost my best instructress.

Excellent schoolmistresses like you don't grow on trees, you know. What am I to do?"

Rochford stopped in his tracks with twinkling eyes. "Write more advertisements, of course. I shall help you with that."

Edmund and Ellen held hands, as if supporting each other.

Miss Hilversham looked at them severely. "You are truly married now?"

They affirmed.

"And you are happy?"

"Oh, yes." Ellen beamed as she looked at Edmund, who squeezed her hand.

Miss Hilversham studied them silently. Then she took off her glasses. "Then, from all my heart, I am glad that you have found your happiness." Her eyes went to her husband, who cooed at his baby. Her entire demeanour softened. "As I have found mine."

ANNA THE MAID ENTERED, CURTSIED, AND FOLDED HER hands. "Mesdames et milords, begging a thousand pardons for the interruption. But a light nuncheon is served in the dining room. If you would deign to follow me, please."

"I say. She is a housemaid, really?" Edmund whispered to Ellen. "I would have mistaken her for one of the pupils here. Either that, or a countess."

Anna had overheard that. "I am, of course, a housemaid, milord." She folded her hands demurely. "Most definitely."

She curtsied.

~

WHEN A LOWLY HOUSEMAID POSES AS THE SCHOOL'S headmistress to impress a mad Earl, she finds herself entangled in an intricate web of deceit and forbidden love.

Read Anna's story in ***Anna and the Mad Earl.***

~

ACKNOWLEDGEMENTS

Parlour games played an important role in the social culture of Regency house parties in the 1800s. These indoor games provided a form of leisurely entertainment that promoted social interaction and courtship, while displaying wit, intelligence and creativity. Guests enjoyed games such as Blind Man's Buff and Charades, which required teamwork and communication, and games such as Consequences and Tableaux Vivants, which showcased literary and artistic talents. Parlour games were an integral part of these gatherings, contributing to the social culture of the time and fostering a sense of community among the guests.

I owe a debt of gratitude to Holli Jo Monroe for helping me with my research and providing essential insight through her work, *The Proper Guide To Parlor Games*. This book was instrumental in the success of my project.

ABOUT THE AUTHOR

Sofi was born in Vienna, grew up in Seoul, studied Comparative Literature in Maryland, U.S.A., and lived in Quito with her Ecuadorian husband. When not writing, she likes to scramble about the countryside exploring medieval castle ruins. She currently lives with her husband, 3 trilingual children, a sassy cat and a cheeky dog in Europe.

Get in touch and visit Sofi at her Website, on Facebook or Instagram!

amazon.com/Sofi-Laporte/e/B07N1K8H6C

facebook.com/sofilaporteauthor

instagram.com/sofilaporteauthor

bookbub.com/profile/sofi-laporte

Printed in Great Britain
by Amazon